CW00471004

Before the Time Machine

Grousable Books

Before the Time Machine

Published by Grousable Books

ISBN: 979-8-9853027-0-7 (print)
ISBN: 979-8-9853027-1-4 (e-book)
Library of Congress Control Number: 2021924696

1

The story starts in St. Pancras, although maybe it's King's Cross because she could never remember exactly how she got there from the airport. Yes, St. Pancras, out past the food, with a glance over at the police in flak jackets watching everyone who went near the Eurostar waiting area. Somehow she'd crossed the street to the other station. One time she emerged from St. Pancras with her suitcase, the wheels racketing over the pavement, and was completely lost, looking around hopelessly. A kind English woman pointed her across the street to King's Cross.

Inside, a visit to the toilets was essential. It cost 20p then, or was it 30p? She never seemed to have the right change, but usually the gate had been propped open by someone anyway. Through the big lobby where people took photos at Platform 9 3/4 (my goodness how that had expanded into a Disney-style attraction) then out to where other people, real people, stood with their necks craning toward the train boards, waiting to rush onto their train to get a proper seat. Then past the Boots on the corner, where she'd buy codeine pills on her way back, because you couldn't get them in America.

Sometimes in dreams, when she imagined she was in the country, she'd see villages and towns and rivers, but first the station. She always seemed to arrive here, even when trying to avoid it, tired and jet-lagged and hungry. Each time the solution was the Pret out in the courtyard, with the taxi queue always longer and further away than it seemed. The concrete blocks where she ate her smoked salmon sandwich and fruit were always the same, with so many kinds of people sitting or lying on them while a continual river of people passed by, traveling between Gilbert's Victorian monstrosity (now a hotel) and the corner leading up the road. Last time, the path to the corner had been blocked by roadworks, and people didn't like the narrowing of the human river. They did strange things as they got nearer to the corner, yelling out at friends or twisting their bodies so no one would touch them. She saw one man pirouette into the air, an angry pirouette, like a hostile bird. Everyone had to jam up at the crossing rather than the corner, and they moved uneasily, discontented that their normal path was disrupted.

Eventually she joined them, heading up the Pentonville Road to what she hoped was the flat she'd tried to find on Google Maps. Avoiding the temptation to pay hotel prices or rent more space than she needed, she'd paid for a room in someone else's flat, a professional couple. The flat was in a newer building, or refurbished anyway, and had a lot of security. Part of the security, she supposed, was the hidden number on the building, well off the main road. She rang the buzzer.

There was a pause, then "Hi, take the lift, the code is 330, it won't bring you up without the code," then silence. Following instructions, she found the lift and alighted on a dark floor at the top of the stairs, with two doors. Neither had a number. She noticed the door on the left was latched open, and peeked in.

"Hello? It's Katherine."

"Hello," said a young woman. Asian heritage, Katherine thought, but with a London voice. Spotting the rows of shoes blocking the hall, she quickly added hers to the collection. No problem, she thought — this is what we do at home, and it means the floor will be cleaner. Instantly forgetting her hostess's name, she was shown round the flat, to her very small bedroom and bathroom across the hall ("ours is in our room"). Then the main room, flooded with light although it looked out only onto other modern flats. "I work in here all day," said the woman, "but you can put your food in the fridge and come and go as you like — here's the keys." Then she smiled briefly and returned to her desk, which looked out on the huge windows.

The woman began, or resumed really, working on her computer.

Unperturbed that this would obviously not be a comfy welcome with a cup of tea, Katherine took a shower, squeezed her suitcase into the small bedroom, and opened it enough to get out her loafers (so much easier for off and on), laptop and papers. Unsure whether she should interrupt, she called out, "I'm off to the library — see you later" and heard a quiet "ok see you" from the main room.

Back on the street. Back through the crush of people at the corner, her feet rejoicing at the change of shoes after 24 straight hours in her Dr. Scholl's. Passing the Victorian monstrosity and the exits from the Underground spewing out the frantic commuters, she remembered to turn right before the Library. I'll go down this alley to the side entrance, she thought — that's quicker. But on entering the courtyard, she saw a queue. At first there seemed to be just a dozen people, but then looking across the courtyard she noticed the line snaked through, just with more spacing than an American line. Following along the queue, she ended up out the other gate and a ways down the road. Funny, the walk had seemed much closer on the computer.

The queue to get in was long, thin, and quiet. Almost everyone in it was a single person, with a knapsack or tote bag. Silent, patient, shuffling until the entrance. Then security, opening the knapsacks and tote bags, everyone saying thank you for a ritual that was a bit reassuring and a bit invasive. Just like last time, she forgot about the lockers and went up to the Reading Room, only to remember and go down the stairs. Oh, yes, the lockers are tricky. Not all of them work. Some that are open won't close. Many that are closed won't open. And you have to put in the code twice, then take a photo of the locker because there are hundreds. However aware you are when you go in, you won't be after four hours of research.

One time she had forgotten to put in the code twice, and came back hours later to find the locker, but it wouldn't open. She'd had to seek out a young man in a lanyard helping someone else, wait, then beg for help.

Up the two flights of stairs and press the door button. The Reading Room guards often had different accents, seeming to come from other parts of the Commonwealth. They were pleasant but spoke only to each other in between checking everyone's bags carefully, regardless of how many times you went in and out. She'd smile and greet them, but they never smiled back.

∾

She took notes on the article, with Bertie reading over her shoulder. You don't think I was serious when I wrote that, do you?

How would I know? she said. You certainly seem angry here. Kind of sensitive to criticism, if you ask me.

Well, of course I was sensitive, he whispered. I was young, but very well-read, very smart. Had my fill of all those Oxbridge types telling me I wasn't good enough, when I knew more than they did.

∾

Summer 1872

The back garden was terrible, but it was all he knew. It was really more of a yard, with the necessary outbuilding for necessary biological activities. About half the yard was bricked, and half bare ground. The bare ground was soaked with kitchen water and outbuilding overflow. But there was an enormous dustbin. Or it seemed enormous when one was six.

There wasn't much room to play inside the house. The ground floor, facing Bromley High Street, was occupied by the shop. Bertie's father Joseph sold china, pots and pans, and cricket equipment. This was not his original trade, and he had no training for it. He had been a gardener at Uppark, the estate home of the family Fetherstonhaugh (pronounced "Fanshaw") in West Sussex. It was there he had fallen in love with the housemaid, Sarah. They both had dreams above their station, although Sarah was the more pragmatic, pious, and practical.

Joseph was also a cricketer for the Sussex team. Ten years before, against their arch-enemy Kent, he had taken four Sussex wickets in four balls, and altogether nine wickets for forty-two. This extraordinary achievement was frequently mentioned by visitors to the shop. He was astute enough to start stocking cricket equipment in response. Because the shop was small, the living area was stuffed with such equipment, as well as pots and crockery.

Broken pots, crockery, and wickets also piled up in the yard. But the dustbin was usually just full of ashes. These ashes could be arranged into hills and valleys, and a dribble of water could make rivers. Entire wars could take place in the dustbin. Armies on the march, towns under siege, burials of the dead.

If one tried very hard, one could ignore the activities surrounding the yard. The tailor next door, with the chunking sound of the one sewing machine. The haberdasher on the other side, emitting a strong smell of horse manure from his mushroom greenhouse. And the cries of the pigs and sheep awaiting slaughter at the butchers behind the wall. One could, especially if one were six, be miles away, campaigning among the ashes.

∾

She supposed the diagnosis had something to do with it, or maybe it was the return afterward. She'd thought she would die soon, and never see England again, that time she returned. Actually cried on the plane, quietly of course. But then she hadn't died, although the surgery made her tired for years. Death followed her, a continual reminder, a traveling companion. He seemed further away when she came here, or perhaps he was just more content when she was on the move.

She had cleverly invented a research project that required her to come, something with resources unavailable in America. Not wanting to be a tourist (she was born here, after all), she'd focused on getting into the great libraries. The British Library, the Bodleian in Oxford. She'd become a reader, requesting 19th century sources. Writing articles. Writing a book. Investigating.

∾

Shall I tell you how I started a life of autodidacticism? he said.

I have read your autobiography, but I'd certainly rather hear it from you, she said. Something about you breaking your leg?

Yes! Some boy at school picked me up and put me down too firmly. So I had to stay home on the sofa. And my father brought me books from the Bromley Institute.

Your house isn't there anymore, she said.

Oh? Yes, well it wasn't much of a house. Very dark downstairs. Spooky garden. What is there now?

A Primark, she said. A shop with cheap clothes made by children in poor countries.

That, he said, doesn't sound like an improvement. I always said the railway would ruin the place.

Bertie described the many authors he'd read from the books his father had brought him. He seemed quite proud about his father. A great cricketer in his younger days. Took four wickets in four balls. Until he broke his leg, pruning the grapevine in the back garden. Put the whole family in destitution.

Mother had to go back to work. She went back to Uppark, where she had been a maid, to be the new housekeeper. It was so hard on her.

Should I tell you, she said, how your father may really have broken his leg? I found a statement from an interview with one of your neighbors. She said your father was quite the ladies' man. You know how he rarely went to church? He had one of his women over on a Sunday, while your mother went to church with you and your brothers. Something happened and you all returned early. He managed to get his lady friend over the back garden wall, but when he tried to climb up he fell and broke his leg.

Really? he said. We had no idea. Where on earth did you read that?

It was in the Bromley Library catalog of your work. So really, your way with women comes to you honestly.

Wonder who the neighbor was, he said. Must not have liked us very much.

∾

"I won't do it," she said.

"You'll have to. They're going to install a computer on your desk, and they'll all be connected, and you'll get electronic mail."

It was 1995.

"I won't do email unless they take away something else, either regular mail or my telephone. I won't answer three bells."

But she did, of course, three bells all the time. She tried checking her mailbox less, but it didn't help.

Then later. "But I don't know what the internet is," she said.

"Look," her colleague said somewhat impatiently, "it's like all the computers connected together."

"In the world? How? How would that even happen?"

He tried to draw her a picture, little boxes connected together. "I don't understand," she said. "You can't link all the computers in the world together."

Then a few years later, listening to the dial-up tones on the modem, getting her work email from home, it was easy. Then a workshop. The workshop. Not optional, required. The World Wide Web. How to Make a Web Page.

She was hooked. <h1>Welcome to my web page</h1> to make a heading. Then a <p> to make a paragraph. And when you were done, you saw what you'd created on the screen. Like magic. Like all the typewriters and word processing machines she'd ever used, like the Apple IIe she'd written her thesis on. Only better.

And you could add pictures. Little, tiny pictures you had to scan, then compress. Don't let the page take too long to load!

1998. The first three classes she offered "online" over the internet. It's just like our TV courses, the college admins said, but interactive. Instead of mailing papers, students can send them to you by email, and you can send them back.

Things started to go more quickly after that. Discussion boards. Chat rooms. The Read-Write Web. Learning Management Systems. She became an expert at all of them. Late nights chatting with strangers about sex. Daytime workshops, everyone learning how to teach online. A few people exchanging tips while everyone else said it's a fad, it's pulling from real teaching, who wanted to take classes on a computer?

ڪ

I suppose it was like when I started with William Briggs, Bertie said. No one knew what he was doing either. Started small, just tutoring his students by post. Expanded it into a major enterprise, enough to support his family. Correspondence courses to prepare students for London University exams, and civil service exams. Then the residential program in Cambridge, just to be able to put "Cambridge" on the stationery. That's a Yorkshireman for you. I'm from the south, myself.

I know, she said. I've been to your house.

2

She was in a second-hand bookstore, naturally. The phone rang and she half-listened as the proprietor began a conversation.

"Oh, yes, thank you for calling. Yes, it happened about ten days ago. I am surprised not to have heard from you sooner?"

She looked briefly through the titles in her field. She had all of them except one.

"Yes, they took the money from the till. There wasn't much there, since I had taken the day's money to the bank that evening."

Twenty pounds for this one. No, I think not.

"The main thing is, they made a mess. They broke a window. Piles of books were knocked over, paperbound books thrown about."

She looked around. There were books piled on every available surface. Some towered and tilted. There was barely enough room to walk in the aisles.

"Well, no, the alarm didn't go off."

Ah, she thought, they did have an alarm.

"Because we had to turn it off, you see. We already had two notices."

She walked over to look at the education section but could still hear. The main desk was in the center of the shop.

"Well you see, we had this giant rat. He'd run about at night and set off the alarm. The first time the council was nice about it, but the second and third time…"

The piles of books began to look like rat shelters.

"They gave us a limit. Wasting police time and all that. So we were waiting to set the alarm again until the new year."

She'd been in the basement earlier, because that's where the history books were. There had been sounds behind the piles of books, but she'd assumed it was the pipes.

"Yes, I understand. I've blocked up the window with some wood."

She had been about to move one of the piles to look behind but decided not to.

"Of course, you can't be expected to respond if we don't have the alarm on. I just thought there might be something you could do…"

Even the police can't take on the Giant Rat of Guildford, she thought. Not sure I could either.

～

Why on earth would you rename your own wife? she asked. Wasn't it enough that she took your last name? I can't understand how a man like you, who in so many ways appreciated female independence, could do something like that.

She didn't mind, he said. I loved her very much.

～

Her walk up Whitehall was traditional. As a younger historian, she'd been enchanted by the story of Charles I. On her first trip to England when she was eighteen, she'd journeyed out to Portsmouth just to see the house where the Duke of Buckingham was murdered by that Puritan maniac. It was an architect's office now. She went in quietly.

"May I help you?" said the young man, the sleeves of his blazer pushed up like he'd been writing. Drawing, she thought. Architect.

"Yes, please, I'm sorry. I know that this house is where the Duke of Buckingham was killed, and I wanted to see inside."

"You came all the way from America to see where the Duke of Buckingham was killed?" Her accent was obvious. The other man in the room smiled, amused.

"Well, no, but I did come out to Portsmouth today from London, just hoping."

"Would you like to see the room where they brought him? It's upstairs." They were so kind, sending her up and telling her she could stay as long as she liked. Then she'd walked down to the port, and saw a bust of Charles I in a niche in the wall.

Charles had died, martyr to some, tyrant to others. Sentenced to die "with his crown on" by Cromwell and his Rump. She'd been there too, to the Banqueting Hall, imagining Charles coming out the upper window onto the raised scaffold, wearing two hair-shirts under his clothes so he wouldn't be thought to shiver from fear.

The Whitehall walk was just a little bit of pilgrimage then, up from the Houses of Parliament to Trafalgar Square. This time, she thought, I'll stop at a pub. I don't know much about pubs, and I'm on my own, but here surely they'll all be government men after work? Seems pretty safe. Some place on Whitehall, she wanted. Entering she saw the bar and remembered to come up and ask for a beer. Don't sit first. Go up to the bar.

She didn't like beer, really — she liked porter. But she'd been told in Oxford, at the Eagle and Child, that no one drinks porter in the summer. So she ordered one off the tap at the bar, went to the back, and sat down. From there, she could see the other taps, ones she hadn't known were there. One had a porter. She didn't like the beer. It was bland and tasteless. She convinced herself she didn't have to drink it if she didn't like it. Life was too short. Taking the half up to the bar, she asked if she could have the porter instead.

"Look, love, why didn't you ask for a taste?"

He was frowning. Wasted beer. Bloody Americans. She drank her porter, alone at the back.

Bertie wasn't there then. He didn't like walking up Whitehall.

∽

January 1873

Fanny had died from a birthday party. That's what it had looked like, anyway. She went to the party, got a belly ache, and three days later she was dead. It had been before Bertie was born. But he knew all about it, and every January his mother became very sad. Fanny would have been his only sister. He knew the story, but as far as he was concerned the biggest problem was the cod liver oil.

"I don't want to take it," said young Bertie.

"You must," said Sarah. "Look at your brother. He's pigeon-breasted. Why? Not enough cod liver oil. I am not going to let that happen to Frank or to you. Not when I can do something about it."

It had worked for Fanny when she had been very small, turning her from a sickly child into a lively, happy little girl. Sarah would never forget that. There was no getting out of that daily spoonful. He took it, and Sarah smiled that sad, encouraging smile.

"All better," she said. She enfolded him, wrapping her arms around him. Her worn and reddened hands squeezed him. "You are my wonderful little boy," she said. "You've been sent by God to replace my perfect little girl. She was such a delight, helping around the house. Even at only nine years old, she could do so many things." Sarah sniffed.

At seven years old, Bertie knew his mother worked hard and loved him. But he also knew he could never be like Fanny. And he knew that any God who could take Fanny away from Sarah was not a good thing at all.

Sarah wiped her eyes on her apron.

"All right," she said. "Time for your catechism." She took out the list of what he had forgotten last time, and he sat dutifully down at the kitchen table. The kitchen, being underground, was very dark, but she always had a lamp at the ready.

"How many parts are there in a Sacrament?"

"Two."

"What are they?"

"The outward visible sign, and the inward grace."

"Inward spiritual grace," she corrected.

"Inward spirit-ula grace." Might he be able to go outside soon?

"What is the outward visible sign or form in Baptism?"

"Um. Water?"

"Wherein a person is baptized—" she prompted.

"In the name of the Father, and of the Son, and of the Holy Ghost." He grinned.

She didn't smile.

"Last question." Bertie wiggled to be more upright in his chair, and concentrated. Was there a way to make his mother smile?

"What is the outward part or sign of the Lord's Supper?"

Bertie's eyes twinkled. "Bread and butter!"

Instead of a smile, there was a quick intake of breath. She looked down at her hands and closed the book. Bertie's grin vanished as she lowered her voice. It sounded like it came from below the kitchen.

"May God forgive you, Bertie." It dawned on him that he'd done something terrible.

"Go outside." She rose slowly, and took her diary, the new one for the year, from the shelf against the wall. As he left the kitchen, he heard her start to cry.

༄

It's because you're not English, he said.

Well, I was born here, she replied.

Yes, but really you're American.

I prefer Californian, actually.

Will I go to California?

13

I don't know, she said. I'd have to look it up.

∽

Accommodations in Oxford were always challenging. Katherine watched Inspector Morse in "The Wolvercote Tongue" for the third time, thinking how nice it would be to stay at the Randolph in Oxford. Every time she checked the prices, they were higher. It was as if the website waited for her to return so it could laugh at her.

In reality, she planned each trip economically. Airbnb, VRBO, HomeAway. Dorm rooms at universities. For Oxford, it wasn't the Randolph. She booked an Airbnb in Jericho. The owner, Sally, had created a good listing. She was rarely there, she wrote, but the cat was always home and needed to be fed. Katherine wouldn't mind that at all. It would be good to have some feline company. There was a washing machine. The price was right, and the flat equidistant between the Bodleian and the gate into Port Meadow. She was all set.

A week before leaving, an email came from Sally. All the information was there. The keypad code, the rubbish collection schedule. *And Omar shouldn't be around much, so it should be quiet.*

Omar?

He's a graduate student, wrote Sally. *He's no trouble.*

He lives in the flat?

Oh yes, didn't I say?

No, Sally had not said there was a man living in the flat. Katherine wrote that she felt the listing should have mentioned this. Instead, the listing had made it sound as though it was just Sally, and she wouldn't be there. Nowhere did it say there was an Omar living upstairs.

Katherine sat down to play contradictions with her conscience. Surely Omar would be perfectly nice. He was a graduate student at Oxford. She should not be afraid of being in the flat with Omar and the cat.

The first episode of Morse was a woman being killed in Jericho.

That's ridiculous. It's a book and a television program. It's not real.

Murder is real.

Maybe I'm just afraid because his name is Omar. Would I be afraid of a Jack?

Yes, I think so. I don't know this person.

You don't know Sally either.

True.

The whole thing is really scary, when you think about it.

I said I wouldn't be scared of things anymore.

But I am.

Well, I can't afford the Randolph.

Fine. I'll get a room at student housing. Uncomfortable but safe.

Nothing's safe...

She'd known it would be a bit confusing to find the room, especially in such hot weather. The office to check in was right near Carfax Tower, where the busses turned. She'd managed to get her bag off the bus near the corner. It was almost lunchtime. Sweating tourists, mostly Chinese, crowded the pavement. Some pushed down Aldgate toward Christ Church, to visit the cathedral. Through the window of the corner shop, she could see them buying grey sweatshirts with the maroon Oxford logo printed on them. They cost £70. She couldn't even imagine buying one.

She went into the Aldgate office, inside the Town Hall, looking up at the building as she entered. Those would be nice rooms, she thought. Wonderful building. All that ornamentation on the windows. Mullions, she thought. I love mullions. She went up to the desk. A large fan blew warm air across the room.

"Hello," she said to the student behind the desk. "Is this where I check in?"

The bespectacled young man looked up from the computer. His nose was damp, and she worried his glasses might slide off.

15

"Yes, madam," he said. (When had she gone from miss to madam?) "Nice weather, isn't it?"

"A bit warm," she said. He smiled. There it is, she thought, the British hot weather smile. It must be wonderful because it isn't raining. He pushed a book toward her. "Just sign in here, please."

He pulled open a drawer under the counter. "You'll be in 303," he said. "Just go across the road there, and use this fob on the glass door. The lift is on the left."

She looked across the road at the drab, gray, modern building.

"Across the road?" she said.

"Yes, just there. The glass door, next to the shop. It doesn't look like an entrance, but it is."

It was. To a building that looked like an office block. The air in the lobby was stuffy and still. Up the lift, 303, key in the door. The room was small and went straight back to the window. Katherine pulled the blinds. A courtyard below, with the rubbish bins. Another office block wall straight ahead. The room was stifling. She opened the window. There wasn't a breath of air.

Taking off her shoes, she noticed the carpet was sticky. Everything else seemed clean, so she began to lay things out on the desk. Thank goodness there was always a desk, always with tea things on a little plastic tray. She plugged in her laptop, put her book and mini-torch beside the single bed, put her shoes up off the floor in the wardrobe. Everything off the carpet, she thought. In case of bedbugs.

Even after an hour with the window open, the room was unbearably hot. Sleeping would be impossible, she knew. Perhaps she could buy an electric fan? Something small.

Outside the tourist crush was even worse. She crossed and headed to Boswell's. Right inside the front door was a stack of electric fans. Around the stack people were crowding, rushing to buy one before they ran out. There was no orderly queue, but a bodily mass like a large insect, with tentacles reaching for boxes. She must have looked surprised. A harried clerk came by and said, "Don't worry — there are a few more at the back."

She went to the back and collected a box. At the till, a young woman rang up her purchase. She was wearing a sleeveless blue top, with sweat stains under her arms. I wish I could do sleeveless, thought Katherine. But not a chance.

"Quite a run on the fans," said Katherine.

"Oh, yes," panted the girl. "We're the only place that has any left."

Returning to the airless room, she clipped the fan onto the bookshelf, pointing it at the pillow on the bed. It was a godsend. She sat on the bed and began going through her list for requests at the Bodleian.

∾

May 1880

He could do this examination in his sleep, Bertie thought. And it will be the last thing I do in this awful place.

The schoolroom was as dreary as ever. It hadn't changed much in the almost six years he'd been here. Waiting for the papers, he heard the younger boys sniffling and snickering in their seats. Surely Mr. Morley would be sober on the day of the big bookkeeping exam? But perhaps it didn't matter either way.

Bertie had first arrived at the tender age of seven and three-quarters. He had been frightened. Thomas Morley's Commercial Academy was just up the High Street from his home, but he'd felt very connected to home lately. His broken leg meant he had spent weeks on the sofa, surrounded by various items from the shop. At times he had felt like he might be carted out and sold as a piece of goods. The books he'd read had been so wonderful that he'd almost felt too old for school. Yet there he'd been, pale and small, wearing his woolen apron, carrying a little green satchel. He must have looked quite silly then, he thought.

Now that he was much older, he realized that his mother must have cut up her old dress for him to have a pinafore with pockets. He knew that she'd pinched pennies to send him to this school. The Commercial Academy was not for very poor children. His mother had aspirations. By rights he should have gone to the National School. Under the new law that passed when he was just a baby, elementary education must be provided for all. Small private schools like the Academy were remnants of an earlier time. Sarah felt that if her boys were to move up in the world, become proper clerks in proper businesses, the state-funded school would be unsuitable.

Writing, arithmetic, and history, if there was time, made up the supposed curriculum. But in actuality the Academy was training bookkeepers. Mr. Morley, with his prodigious whiskers, was a task master. Next to his desk, with its giant ink bottle for judicious refilling of the desk wells, was his cane. His use of the cane was unpredictable. Usually, it was wielded with silent and deliberate attention, as the sentence after a considered judgment. But as the years went by, more and more it was used immediately, even for minor infractions. Perhaps it was the drink that caused his anger. Certainly it was the drink that caused him to sleep during the afternoons, when the stove in the center of the room made things nice and cozy. Then he would wake and, certain he'd missed some evil going on, would reach for the cane. Sometimes he'd ignore the cane and reach for anything handy — a book, a ruler — and go after the culprit. He invariably hit the boys' hands, which made further work painful. The striking was often accompanied by verbal abuse, name-calling, words designed to induce shame. They rarely did so. The boys were accustomed to it.

When Morley wasn't up to hitting, there were other punishments. The worst was to be forced to stand in the corner with arms out in front, holding up heavy objects. It was odd, Bertie thought later, that so much punishment was meted out on the limbs needed for the requested tasks. Although certainly the backside was often a target as well.

There were over twenty boys in the one room. Some were Morley's favorites, and they knew it. Others he despised, including several of the boarders who came from unsuitable homes. In the evenings, these boys were Mrs. Morley's problem. Lessons went on in the mornings, and again in the afternoons. The windows were rarely open, and by the afternoon the room was warm and damp and sleepy. Bertie found it difficult to learn anything after mid-day. But he worked hard, realizing that Morley wanted the best for the boys. Even the punishments were his effort to force them into a better future than they would have had without him. He was a trained teacher, a Licentiate of the College of Preceptors. Certainly the teachers at the National School were far worse.

The dingy schoolroom was the same. But the outside world, Bromley High Street, had changed since Bertie began school here. The train lines to the south were being extended. The independent town was becoming half suburb, half gateway to the south of England. While Morley snoozed, the boys told each other stories, played marbles, shared crude jokes. When awake, Morley strictly enforced the way to hold the pen, the correct way to do sums, the methods for preparing for the College's examinations. All his boys would earn certificates, or he would know the reason why. They would go out in this expanding world and make their way. Bertie wanted to make his mother proud and be worthy of the money she'd spent on him. He'd rather tell the boys more stories — he had many to tell. But he'd hold his pen correctly and pass this examination.

3

Midhurst is a small town in West Sussex, on the bus line to the West Sussex Records Office in Chichester. Katherine had seen Chichester in an episode of *Rosemary and Thyme* and was happy to go there. But Midhurst was the main goal, since it was where Bertie had become a pupil-teacher after an unhappy stint as a draper's apprentice.

As an isolated scholar, Katherine did not have many connections anywhere, and the one she had in Midhurst was based on a commercial transaction. In studying Bertie's first book, *The Text-book of Biology*, she had decided she wanted a copy.

The little book had first been in her hands the year before, and she was enchanted by its small size and fold-out illustrations. Getting the book into her hands had not been easy. She'd found it in the Bodleian Catalog. On her first visit to the Bodleian, she had been charmed by the personal process of getting a Readers Card, including the taking of the Bodleian oath. This promised to do no harm to the books, and it had to be said aloud to the librarian. After this, she asked about access to the Oxford Union to see the book.

She was told that was most unusual, since the Oxford Union was only for members. However, the librarian was very kind and offered to "call over" to see if they could accommodate her. They said yes, so that's how she ended up walking through the pedestrian mall, past Carfax Tower, loads of tourists, and unemployed men who yelled rude things at her. Coming upon the stunning old building, she entered to find the desk.

Now Oxford Union's library is not necessarily famous for its books alone. Katherine knew they had paintings done by the pre-Raphaelites somewhere, and she very much wanted to see them. That had been the main reason she requested to see the book here, rather than the Bodleian proper.

The librarian retrieved the book for her, and she was pointed into the library, replete with rich furnishings and mullioned windows. Turning the volume over in her hand, she'd been delighted that it did actually seem small enough for a working man to carry with him. This was important, since it was for learning by correspondence. Working people cannot always have time at home to study.

Taking some photos with her mobile phone, she looked around the room, then decided to ask the question about the paintings. She inquired at the front desk. The librarian looked confused.

"But," she said, "you've just been in there with the paintings."

"I have?"

"Yes, just look up," she said, taking Katherine's two pound viewing fee apologetically. Back into the room and, sure enough, they were up near the ceiling, there the whole time. She climbed the narrow stairs for a better look. Then she returned to the desk.

"Delightful," she said. "It's silly, but scholars don't always look up."

Upon her return to America, with a birthday coming, she'd gotten onto a used book website and found a $200 copy of the 2nd edition of the text-book, and bought it. An email reply came the next day from the owner of the bookshop, saying he'd ship the book soon. Did she know it was coming from Midhurst, where Bertie himself had lived and gone to school? She did indeed, and a brief correspondence began with the bookshop owner.

Once in Midhurst, they had met for tea, and he'd shown her around Roman ruins no one knew were there, told her about the Roman artifacts in people's basements, showed her the Roman stonework under the shop. "Really," she said, "you should have house tours of this stuff."

"Good idea," he said. "And when you publish your book, we'll proudly carry it."

∽

February 1881

Bertie was so pleased to be pupil number 33. His mother had agreed to sign the application, seeming to accept the fact that her son would not be a chemist. True, the Latin had been a problem. It was difficult to help at a chemist's when you didn't know your arnica from your aconite. He had loved the shop, with its exotic glass bottles and the little rolling frame for pills. Samuel Cowap the chemist, upon learning of his deficiency in Latin, sent him to evening classes with Horace Byatt.

Byatt was the new headmaster for Midhurst Grammar School. The trouble was, there was no school yet. It was being rebuilt after a fire, and many years dereliction. Surely, thought Cowap, Byatt could teach his young apprentice enough Latin to be useful.

Bertie quickly realized that Byatt himself was enthusiastic but didn't know much Latin either. But he was astonished by his 14-year-old pupil. Surely a lad who could blast through Smith's *Principia* and Euclid's geometry in such short order would be useful at the school. Eager to show both thrift and enthusiasm, Byatt wanted to establish pupil-teachers who could assist with the younger boys.

When the youth decided he could not afford the proper education to be a chemist, and he knew his mother could not, he left the chemist's shop. His mother, recently re-established at Uppark as the housekeeper, could not decide what to do. Bertie suggested he stay at school, and Byatt was happy to approve an application if Sarah would sign it. Until the school was built, young Bertie could stay with Byatt's family in his house at South Pond.

But Byatt had another motive in wanting young Bertie. With his extraordinary ability to learn books at one reading, the boy could take the examinations.

"What examinations?" asked Bertie.

"The Education Department examinations," explained Byatt. "I will provide you with special classes in the evening, after school. Then you take exams. When you do well, the school gets more money. It will help earn your keep, and you'll learn a great deal."

Bertie agreed, eager to learn as much as he could. He quickly discovered that the "special classes" were comprised of him and a book or two, studying at the desk while Byatt dozed in a chair. He didn't mind. Byatt acquired textbooks in physiography and anatomy. Bertie studied them and took the exams. By the end of two months, he had earned grant money for the school, and was excited by every subject he encountered.

His mother, however, was not. It was all very well to be earning his keep, but he needed to get a real start in life. Books, she felt, would not do that. She sent him as a draper's apprentice to Mr. Hyde's Drapery Emporium in Southsea.

∽

Yes, I lived here, he said as they walked down the High Street, plagued with motorcycles because it was Sunday. With Mr. Byatt, at first, before they'd finished rebuilding the Grammar School.

But which house, she asked, because I've been trying to find it.

She had been trying, hard.

∽

Uppark was not easy to get to. It couldn't have been for Bertie either, and yet he came often.

For Katherine, it was a train to Petersfield, then a wait for a bus. She had a little time to walk before the bus came and noticed a plaque on a pub near the main square. It claimed that Bertie had written there often. That can't be right, she thought — he only ever came through here, even when visiting his father in Liss. I wonder if they know it's not true. I wonder if they care.

The bus dropped off at the base of the drive to Uppark House and Gardens (National Trust). No pavement, no space, climb the hill before cars come along and smash you. First stop should clearly be what the British called the "lower ground floor," where Bertie's mother had worked as housekeeper. Some scholars claimed the dark underground world he'd later written about was based on these passages, which were used by servants. Bits of sunlight, more than Katherine had expected, shined in openings at the tops of the passages, near the ceilings. But the outside world could not be seen except for the sky.

She visited the housekeeper's room, where his mother Sarah had worked, and saw the enlarged reproduction of her son's application to the Grammar School. As she went upstairs, even though it was not as interesting as below, they closed the downstairs, saying there weren't enough volunteers. Upstairs, talking to one of the docents about her work, she was asked to stay and be a guide. "I can't," she said. "I have to go back and teach in America."

Outside the grounds were so lovely she actually drew a picture. She hadn't drawn really since she was a child. In high school, she had taken an art class. She did her best, but she wasn't very good. The teacher explained why, by drawing two brains on a chalkboard. "This," he said pointing to the larger one, "is a boy's brain and this," he said pointing to the smaller, "a girl's brain. And that's why girls can't do art." Even at fourteen, even knowing perfectly well that girls can do anything boys can do, she couldn't bear to draw.

On her way out, she stopped at the ice cream stand. Knowing how proprietary the English are about their counties (which she had experienced trying to get a bus from one to another), she made a joke. Noticing that the ice cream came from Hampshire, she said, "Oh! Imported!"

She thought she was being funny. They thought she was being American. She stood by the road in the tall grass, being nibbled by midges, until the bus came.

∽

I came back to Uppark so often because I was ill, said Bertie. I also missed my mother, although I didn't write about that. Not suitable for a boy, you know.

But mostly, he said, I loved the library. Sir Harry Fetherstonhaugh had died in 1846, but many of his books and things were still in the house. His young wife and her sister kept everything as it was, pretty much. The library had books with the writings of Plato, and Voltaire in French so I could learn the language. I read Thomas Paine and *Gulliver's Travels*. I wasn't allowed to actually read in the library, but the sisters let me borrow them. I'd take them back to my room and read them at night when I should have been sleeping.

The attic was magical too. It was next door to my bedroom at the top of the house. I found books of engravings by Raphael and Michelangelo and took careful note of any women who were nude. There was a telescope and other instruments in the attic. No one had touched them in years. At first it just looked like brass pieces in a box, but I put them together. I studied the stars.

Uppark gave me a lifelong love of culture. Later on, even when I promulgated socialist ideas, I realized the value of the wealthier classes. Their role was to preserve culture for everyone, to pay for its maintenance and storage. Without their money, their libraries and galleries, our heritage would be lost.

And those underground passages were educational too. One Christmas, a maid named Mary kissed me there. I kissed her back.

I know, Katherine said. A roué and a scholar.

⤚

Katherine loved archives, going in and receiving very old things, tied in bundles with cloth strips. Laying them out on wedges so as not to bend the spines too much. Using gloves, and little ropes to hold down pages. But everywhere was different.

At Chichester little slips of paper were important. Even if no one was there, these needed to be filled out and put in the box. Then there would be a pause, and the person sitting at the desk, who'd been sitting there the whole time, would look up as if in surprise, and take the slip out. Then the same person would disappear in the back, and just when you thought they'd gone for tea, would bring out the bundle.

The bundle wasn't much help. She was able to get minutes of meetings for opening the Grammar School in Midhurst and read the financial reports. But they didn't mention the name of the housemaster they were funding. She knew this was Horace Byatt, in whose house Bertie had stayed. The house address wasn't given in any of the sources. South Pond, was all. Near or overlooking South Pond. Facing South Pond, said Geoffrey West. This would be 1881. She'd walked the road near South Pond. Nothing faced it, exactly, but there were some houses near it, and two where the pond might have been seen out the upstairs windows. The trees. They'd have been smaller, of course. Or different trees.

She approached an intern and told her what she knew. She had the census copies, obtained by a librarian who had a source back home. The question was which way the census taker went on the street. The intern said we have old maps, so let's look. It took hours, with the intern carefully taking out broad sheets of maps and laying them on the table. Some Katherine could take

26

photographs of, but for others it was not allowed. She came out no more certain of which house was Byatt's than she'd been when she came in.

∽

Back in America, she'd put together a packet of the evidence, and given it to her students. "Let's be historians," she said. "Where is Horace Byatt's house?"

They thought she knew, and that it was a test. She said I don't know. This is my research. I'm trying to figure out which house was his. Which way did the census taker walk? You can help me with my work.

They didn't believe her. Working in groups, they each made a guess, but none were based on the census or the map she'd given them.

4

It was a very long walk, and at the halfway point, Bertie thought he should turn back. Would it even do any good, walking all the way to Uppark? Could he make his mother understand?

He was a man now, he knew. She should listen to him. But he was still the baby. Frank and Fred had done what she wished. He had visited Frank in Godalming, hoping to get support. He had written all of them: Frank, Fred, his father. At first his father seemed supportive, until he'd found out about the cost. Then he'd supported Sarah. Bertie had to stay in Southsea, at the draper's Emporium. Finish his indentured apprenticeship, become a good clerk.

But Bertie couldn't be a good clerk. The conditions were appalling, the food horrible, the learning opportunities almost nil. He was about to turn seventeen. Other boys would be finishing school, heading out into the world with better prospects than he had. Why? Because they had money? No, he thought, it wasn't just that. Because they'd had a proper education, not what I've been doing. For almost two years, the *Chambers Encyclopedia* on the Emporium's bookshelf had been his main source of knowledge.

He was hungry. Ignoring breakfast, he'd simply headed out to walk the seventeen miles to confront his mother.

Remembering how happy he'd been in Midhurst as a pupil-teacher, he'd written also to Horace Byatt at the Grammar School. Could he use an usher or assistant teacher at the school? Even if Byatt answered, it was unlikely he'd be able to offer enough to make up for leaving his indenture with Mr. Hyde.

I'm suffering, thought Bertie. I'll tell her I can't take it anymore. Aren't those the people she likes, the Christians who suffer? Except, that's the problem. I'm not even sure I believe in God, but I certainly don't believe in the church. And they want me confirmed — mother, Mr. Hyde, all of them. A vast conspiracy to confirm something I don't believe in. I won't do it. Any of it.

She let me out of working for Cowap, the Midhurst chemist. I wasn't suited, he said. Nor am I to drapery, but she just won't believe it. I'll tell her that's the end of life for me, that I'll drown myself if she won't cancel my contract with Hyde. Southsea. The ocean is right there. I'll just walk into the ocean.

By the time he arrived at Uppark, Bertie was exhausted. He saw his mother coming back from church, down the path. Jumping out from behind a tree, he gave a cry, and her hand flew to her chest. What on earth was he doing here? He must go back at once.

But he wouldn't leave until he'd said his piece, which took over an hour. She sent him back with lunch and train fare, promising to think about it. He was obviously desperate.

Returning to Southsea, he stared at the walls of the cellar where the draper's assistants lived. I will get out of here, he thought. He penned more letters, again to his father, and again to Horace Byatt.

∽

What if I can't get this book done? she said. This is so hard with my teaching load and family responsibilities.

But you must, he said. You must tell my story.

Don't be ridiculous, she said. Everyone's told your story. They were writing your biographies when you were still alive. You're a biographical slut.

He laughed.

～

June 1883

"I shouldn't worry about it," said Horace Byatt, "but it's such a painful letter."

"Let me see it," said Elizabeth, shifting her great bulk. The weather was warm, and she was uncomfortable.

Elizabeth Allin was the wife of the ironmonger, and her son John had been one of the pupils at the Grammar School. She'd known Bertie as her son's pupil-teacher. She'd liked the young man, and had been sad to see him leave.

"Yes," she said, looking over the letter, "he seems quite miserable as a draper's apprentice. I can't imagine what his mother was thinking."

"He wrote me a few weeks ago, asking if there was a role for him at the school, an usher or something. I told him he could be useful. But I can't pay him, of course."

There was a clattering and Frederick entered the kitchen.

"Hello, Mr. Byatt," he said. He took off his cap automatically. Respect for teachers ran in the family.

"Frederick," said Byatt, "I've heard from young Herbert. Not sure what to do, though."

"Well then," said Frederick, "I'm sure Lizzie will help sort it out. I'm off to the market in Haslemere." He kissed his wife, putting his hand gently on her belly. The twins had been lost not long before. He no longer cared whether this one was a boy or a girl.

"Look, Horace," Elizabeth said, "why can't you pay him? I've never seen anyone learn from books the way that boy could. He's obviously in a terrible state. You have assistant masters, don't you?"

"I have one," he said, "but Harris has experience. Bertie was only with me for a couple of months, and that was almost two years ago. He's on a path to be a clerk, his mother says."

Elizabeth smiled. Poor Horace. It was so clear what ought to be done.

"Write him again," she said. "Make an offer, say, £20 a year? Better, if his mother isn't satisfied, offer £20 to start, then £40 later if he stays a full year."

Byatt walked down Knockhundred Row, then up North Street to the Grammar School, thinking. He passed by the sweet shop and waved to Mrs. Walton. Bertie could share with Harris, he thought, in the rooms above her shop. Maybe this could work.

$\backsim$

It's just an airplane, people said. But it wasn't just an airplane.

Katherine first flew in the A380 by accident; it just happened to be the plane assigned to her flight. She also happened to be seated in the upper deck near the window, which could be reached across a wide bin that held everything she'd brought. The lid of the bin also provided a place to lean over and put her head down, a luxury on an eleven-hour flight.

She noticed the seats weren't uncomfortable, that there seemed to be enough space. The bathroom was usually available when she needed it, or at least the queue wasn't very long.

I'm just enchanted, she thought, because they brought pots of tea. No teabags or consternated looks when she wanted tea instead of coffee. Just a regular round of tea. The other Americans had to wait for coffee.

She had booked next summer's flight on the A380, being careful to choose the flights with that plane. A few weeks later she received an email from the airline, saying the times of the flights had been changed. Looking them up, she discovered they were on 747s. This wouldn't do at all.

The hold for calling British Airways was twenty minutes. Then finally, "Hello welcome to British Airways how may I help you?" said a subcontinental voice.

"Thank you," said Katherine. "I need to change my flights, please."

"Yes, I can take care of that for you. What is your confirmation number?"

"WAX259RQ."

"All right. I see here that you have the return from Los Angeles to London. Is that correct?"

"Yes."

"Very good. So do you want to change to different dates?"

"No."

"Very good. So do you want to change to different times on these dates?"

"No. I want to change to a different plane."

"I'm sorry, ma'am." There was a pause. They're assessing my level of sanity, she thought.

"Which plane would you like?"

"The A380. I want to fly on whatever flights that day are on the A380 airplane."

There was a long pause. "May I have you wait for a few minutes?"

"Sure." A pause and silence, then crackly classical music. Katherine surfed the net while she waited, looking up the A380 online. She found Captain Dave on Twitter. He was a pilot of the A380 working for British Airways, and he loved the plane. Wrote about how well it handled, how its air system circulated the air more times per hour than other planes, how the ratio of people to toilets was so good. How it adjusted to turbulence to make it almost unnoticeable. He even had videos from the cockpit.

"Hello, ma'am? You want to change the flights on the same day. I am looking into what the charge should be for that."

"There shouldn't be a charge. You changed the flights, not me. I booked on the A380."

"Yes, ma'am. But that flight has been changed. We can put you at a different time, but I need to check on the charge."

"Look, you shouldn't charge me. You moved the plane."

"We adjusted the flight time, ma'am. May I have you wait for a few minutes?"

This went on for some time, but Katherine was able to obtain permission to switch to the A380, at far less convenient times, without charge. It took over an hour on the phone. I'm an A380 fan, she thought, do or die.

~

March 1884

To say that Bertie hadn't wanted to be confirmed in the Anglican Church was an understatement. He was disgusted by the whole idea. Perhaps it was the influence of Plato, who had represented a pre-Christian world. Or perhaps it was just that he had a strong distaste for hypocrisy.

He had achieved his goal of returning to Midhurst to begin his career as a scholar, or at least as an assistant teacher. His mother had finally agreed to end his indenture at Southsea. But he should have realized that his religious status, unconfirmed in the Church of England, was a liability. Schoolmasters, however lowly, had to be members. And his own mother was a pious woman who had never understood her son's resistance.

Bertie wasn't sure he understood either. It may have been simply strength of character, refusing to bend to a higher power of whose position he was unsure. But mostly, it was the idea of falsehood. Bertie was a young man of truth. He said what he thought most of the time, and he knew he did not believe what he was supposed to believe. But what had been the use of his long walk to free himself if he gave up on such a seemingly minor point?

That's what he told himself. But it didn't feel minor. While certainly unafraid of divine retribution, he was profoundly uncomfortable at a social demand that forced people like him to lie. If he said he believed, he was surely lying, and in public. The whole point of confirmation was that it be a public declaration.

But the time had come, and he was keenly aware that without the proper procedure he could lose his whole future. Horace Byatt was a kind man, but he'd been astonished that Bertie had not met what seemed to be the minimum requirement. Bertie felt caught between his mother and Byatt, and he knew that neither understood. He had pushed around the questions as gently as he could with the kindly curate. Without protesting at all, he had characterized all the teaching as things he was supposed to know how to say. This made it seem better, more like a theatrical conning of lines rather than a declaration of inner belief.

Why was it necessary to sin in order to be accepted into the Church? How could the Church accept members when God knew they didn't believe? And how could any of this be necessary for his new post, teaching science? It wasn't like he was claiming expertise in theology.

Even after the ceremony at Midhurst Parish Church, Bertie was obliged to participate in an encore performance at the church in Harting, much closer to Uppark. This was so his mother could attend. She had never been happier, he saw. For Sarah was not a happy woman. She was a hard-working, dedicated, principled woman whose belief led her to church contentedly every Sunday. How she had raised a boy who called himself "atheist" she could not imagine. But it no longer mattered. His baptism was confirmed by his own words, said in public. He could not go back on them.

She was profoundly grateful to Horace Byatt. He had insisted on this confirmation, and he had sweetened his offer of a post to make it possible for her to cancel Bertie's indenture. Byatt had agreed to £20 the first year, then £40.

Bertie knew he could make this good by taking examinations again to earn grants for the school. He had done it as a pupil-teacher, and he could do even better as an assistant master. His room above the candy shop, next to the Angel Inn, was ideal. Mrs. Walton loved cooking and loved feeding a hungry and appreciative young man. He'd never had so much food given to him, and he began to outgrow his embarrassing thinness. He tried not to think that he'd traded his soul for stews and custard.

∽

"I'm going to devise a Universal Diagram," said Herbert (he didn't want to be called Bertie now that he was at college). "It will explain all phenomenon by the process of deduction." The other young men grumbled and guffawed. Some raised their eyes to the ceiling. Except you couldn't see the ceiling for all the smoke.

"There he goes again," said one of them.

Herbert was only here because he had done well in his work for Horace Byatt at the Midhurst Grammar School. In fact, he had done too well. His examinations had caught the eye of the College of Preceptors' scholarship committee, and he had been granted a three-year full scholarship to the Normal School of Science. He had never dreamed of such a thing; nor had Mr. Byatt, who was miserable at losing him. The Normal School was where T. H. Huxley taught, where science teachers were trained under the keen eye of experts.

It had been a difficult day, trying to study in the cramped flat. Herbert's collar was fraying (why did he get the celluloid one in the first place?) and he hadn't really had enough to eat. But there was always tea at the Debating Society, and it would just have to do until he met up with Jennings later. Jennings always paid, sorry that Herbert never had any money.

∽

Then there was the Bradlaugh-Besant trial. While it wasn't the trial of the century, said Herbert, it was very important to me.

Why? said Katherine. I've never heard of it.

35

It was in all the papers. It must have happened when I was about eleven years old, but I didn't hear about it till I was almost eighteen. There was this book, you see. *Fruits of Philosophy,* by a doctor named Charles Knowlton. Had been around for decades. But there was a lot of information in it about sex, and how to control family size. Some puritanical government minister, persuaded by the Society for the Suppression of Vice, made a case out of it. So Henry Cook, the bookseller, was charged with printing obscene pictures. He went to prison for two years.

That's like Oscar Wilde, said Katherine. Two years for a moral infraction.

Exactly. But two free-thinkers, Charles Bradlaugh and Annie Besant, were angry about it. They began to republish and distribute the book themselves. They even updated the medical information. But the real problem was that they sold it for sixpence. Word got around, and they sold hundreds of copies immediately. They were arrested, and the case went to trial.

So people who'd never heard of the book read about the case?

Precisely, said Herbert. And the story was everywhere, in all the papers. Everyone was talking about it. The only reason I didn't know about it was that my mother wouldn't bring the papers into the house, and the boys at Morley's school didn't read anything. But I learned about it later at the Normal School, when I was out on my own. I borrowed a copy and read all about how to prevent pregnancy. Internal washing with acidic solutions, for example.

So you applied it at once? said Katherine, smiling knowingly.

Oh no, I couldn't. But it taught me that I could. That if I did meet women, and had relations with them, I need not make them pregnant. It opened up a whole world to me. I felt free, being forearmed like that. And I felt that out there were women who were also free.

I don't think, said Katherine, that would be considered a very feminist point of view these days.

But for me, said Herbert, it defined free love. And I was no longer afraid of being intimate with women.

∽

December 1884

The pass list was out at last. And there it was:

>>>*Biology, Part One, Division One: First Class, H. G. Wells*

The first thing was to tell Jennings. "Well, of course!" said Jennings. "You worked so hard."

"I didn't work that hard," said Herbert. "I just love Huxley's lectures."

"But there were only three of us who got a first," said Jennings. "Didn't you see the long list of seconds?"

The two men were walking out of the Normal School building, leaving its large, ornate brick facade behind them. Jennings was slim and usually wore gray. Herbert was also slim but usually wore brown. Unlike Jennings, his slenderness was not the result of an elegant physique. One might call him scrawny.

Herbert had occasionally felt faint, but he had never actually fainted from hunger. He had seen one fellow go down, though, right there in the laboratory. Like him, the one guinea a week hadn't gone far enough. Wells himself usually had only a few shillings left for food after paying rent and such. The Normal School had offered the scholarship, but they didn't seem to understand the physical situation of young men like himself. He had no other means of support than the stipend. His mother occasionally sent him some food, but it wasn't much. He was there, he knew, to learn, not to eat. But he never quite understood why the Normal School wasn't taking care of him in the way he expected. The opportunity was there, but not the means.

Jennings, only a year older, had befriended young Wells. He was trained in the classics, and their conversations helped Wells put together the bits and pieces he had read into a sort of education. Perhaps, he thought, my mind is rough, but I can polish it on Jennings's mind. Besides, he finds me amusing. I tend to joke poorly when I'm nervous, but Jennings thinks I'm witty. He isn't offended by my blasphemous talk, my instinctive irreverence.

"Let's go to the Grill Room in the museum and celebrate your success," said Jennings. Herbert didn't answer. "My treat, of course," said Jennings. "We can order from the third-class menu, if you like."

"Oh no, you mustn't keep paying for me," said Wells. "Let me have some self-respect."

"Don't be daft," said Jennings. "It's an investment."

"An investment?" said Wells.

"In my own intellectual skills," said Jennings. "Look, we're in competition, you see? We're jostling for the same position in life, taking examinations on the same knowledge. If you're ill-fed, you can't hold up your end. I buy you dinner, and that makes the competition more fair. Besides," continued Jennings, "you're lying about not working hard. I see you in the Education Library all the time."

"That's because it's too far to go back to my lodgings and study," said Wells, "and it's much too noisy and cold there."

"It's certainly cold tonight," said Jennings. "Let's order a hearty joint with veg and pudding."

∽

He twinkled his eyes at her.

Stop that, she said. Then, haughtily, I prefer to date people from my own century.

That, he said, has never been true.

5

March 1886

"Shhhh, we're making too much noise," whispered Simmons, as Wells tripped on the corner of a rolling cart. It was darker in the specimen room than outside in the bright afternoon.

"They'll all be at lunch," said Wells softly. There was a clunk on the other side of the apparatus table. "Careful with the camera!"

"So where's the beast, then?" said Simmons. Physics and chemistry were his fields, not biology.

"Just here," said Wells. He was standing in the gloom, and it looked like he had a companion. Simmons began to set up the tripod.

The gorilla skeleton stood as proudly as it could on its stand, with a metal rod running up the middle of its body. Its head came to about Wells' shoulder.

"I can't take a photograph in that corner," said Simmons. "It's too dark. Can we move him more toward the center of the room?"

The two young men together carefully lifted it along with the base and moved it forward into the light. The bones rattled and swayed a bit. They got the stand down squarely. Simmons jumped behind the camera and looked through.

"How should I stand?" said Wells. He looked at the gorilla. The gorilla looked back.

"Put your arm around his shoulder," said Simmons.

"How do you know it's a he?" smiled Wells. "But I can't get around its waist, anyway." He posed.

"We need more," said Simmons. "It's good, but too plain. And we can't make a statement about evolution with just you and him."

"Why not? He represents the foolishness of the anti-Darwinists, and I am the physical manifestation of human perfection."

Simmons snorted. "Be that as it may, some won't understand."

"Fine," said Wells, as he caught sight of the row of skulls along the cabinet. He grabbed one and posed, one arm around the gorilla, the other holding the skull. He turned his gaze to the skull, like Hamlet.

"No, no," said Simmons. "You should look at your companion."

"Very well. I'm quite sure it's a female. I shall gaze adoringly into her … eye sockets."

"Hold still." A click.

∽

You aren't just writing your first book? he said. I wrote books when I was very young.

I know, said Katherine. I have a reprint of *Desert Daisy*.

Oh, I so enjoyed writing that. All the illustrations. That's the one with the king, and someone corrupt who gets his comeuppance, isn't it?

It is. I wrote books when I was a child, too, she said. One was on foolscap, stapled together. I did illustrations too. It was called *Jeannette, Machina, and the Red Colt*.

Hmmm, he said. My title was better.

∽

October 1885

William Briggs and his young wife Ada had been pleased. The announcement had arrived two years before. William had obtained a Professorship in Science at St. Benedict's College, on the shores of Loch Ness. This was despite the fact that he had graduated from the new Yorkshire College of Science, which did not offer full degrees. Ada, who had been a waitress, had just lost their first baby. She was happy for the diversion and the move, happy her husband was moving up in the world. She would, however, miss her family. William, son of a prosperous Leeds stonemason and an ambitious mother, would only miss one thing: the pupils at Leeds Church Middle-Class School.

He had been a pupil-teacher when he attended there as a child. Even after he moved on to the college, he worked as the school's mathematics teacher. Plus he continued to tutor those who needed it. He'd been coaching them privately, preparing them for the examinations in mathematics at the University of London. Now he'd be far away, in Scotland.

Once they had arrived, the energetic William had found his new job interesting but rather ordinary. Fort Augustus wasn't as exciting as Leeds. And he got letters from the old school, asking could he help with just this one problem? And this one too? He decided to tutor by correspondence and set up a fee plan. It was just the same as being a private tutor in Leeds, except he was in Scotland. Poor Ada went back to Leeds for over six months, tending to their sickly second child with the help of her family, and he had some time to establish his scheme.

It made sense, really. There were few tutors available for the mathematics and science examinations. London University provided such an extraordinary opportunity to earn a degree by studying on your own, then taking the examinations. He wasn't sorry he'd attended Yorkshire College, for it had been years ahead in scientific education. It was very progressive. But the degree — that's what young people needed, especially to be more highly paid as teachers. They needed his help.

Letters began to come from other pupils, too. Could he tutor them for the Intermediate in Arts? Not everyone wanted science and mathematics. William knew he couldn't do it. Ada, who had returned saddened by the loss of their second child, couldn't do it. But he knew others at St. Benedict's who could. Perhaps they would be interested in joining his scheme? It could become lucrative.

"Are you doing better, dear?" he asked Ada as they sat with their tea.

"A little," she said. "We'll try again, won't we?"

"Of course." He sighed. "I have gotten more letters asking for Arts tutoring, you know."

"Yes," she said, "it seems you're really making this into a business." He looked at her pale face. More money might mean better doctors.

"I am," he said, "and why not? Everything seems set up for it. We have the penny post for papers, and more people go to London every year to take examinations. There's a demand for teachers, and it can't be met without scholars from all over."

"I'll help, dear," said Ada. "I'll do the typing and contact students. I can take out advertisements in some of the papers. You work on getting more tutors."

"Done," said William. He smiled into her eyes and took her hand.

∼

The bus to Ripon meant a change at Harrogate. So Katherine needed a day pass, for which she had to explain she wanted to go to Ripon. As usual, the bus driver looked confused.

She quickly discovered that the correct pronunciation was "Rippin" as in Rippin' Yarns, not Ri-pawn. Oh, dear, she thought. The locals must have thought she was trying to sound posh. Not that an American ever really sounds posh. She recalled the time she'd seen a beautiful village in a travel catalog. It was called Castle Combe, in the Cotswolds. All these visits, and she'd never been to the Cotswolds. She'd gotten close once, when she went out to Bleinheim Palace from Oxford. Such a long walk from the bus stop by the gate. Coming to the back of the monstrously large building, there had been an event of some kind being set up, ruining the 18th century effect.

Once on the grounds at Blenheim, she was overcome by the wealth and self-aggrandizement. The boat house had the family's name carved above it as if anyone could possibly not know who owned it. There were miles of pretend wilderness, gardened within an inch of its life by Capability Brown. Waterfalls with metal pipes, perfectly round rose gardens. It was too much before she even got in the building, and then the ostentation had been truly ridiculous. She'd decided to leave, take the bus north from Woodstock, and find the village on the brochure. But she remembered the name wrong.

"Is this the bus to Combe?" she asked the driver. She was quite sure she was pronouncing the name wrong.

"Where, dear?"

"Coooombe?" she said, desperately guessing.

"Oh yes, you must want Coom. Come on up."

After only a few miles the bus went through what looked like a small, suburban development. The driver pulled up at the stop. "Here you are, miss. Are you sure this is where you want to be?" She must have looked as tentative as she felt.

"I think so," she lied, embarrassed. "I'm meeting a friend here . . . she said Combe." Katherine hated being caught out making stupid mistakes. She got off the bus. Walking around the nondescript place for an hour, she had no choice but to cross the street to the other bus stop and hope it wasn't the same driver. It was, of course.

Cathedrals are not interchangeable. Ripon was Norman-Gothic transition and was said to have impressive misericords. Despite the fact that she'd begun as a medievalist, Katherine had not known what a misericord was, or whether the word was singular or plural. Apparently they were ledges under seats that flipped up, to support your behind when you were standing during the service. Some featured wood carvings under certain seats, instead of a plain ledge or protrusion. She'd sat on folded seats before in choir stalls. Even at large cathedrals and churches, there were usually few people there for Evensong, unless you were at Christ Church, Cambridge. She'd almost been trampled by a group of Chinese tourists there, and no longer attended. Everywhere else, there were so few people that worshipers sat in the choir stalls, behind and next to the choir singers.

At Ripon, one misericord carving was of a rabbit being chased down a hole by a fox. Charles Dodgson's father had been a canon at the cathedral. A story had sprung up of young Charles, later known as Lewis Carroll, looking at that misericord and getting the idea for the white rabbit. This one certainly looked to be in a hurry. Katherine felt she knew Dodgson a little. She had been brought up with the big annotated volume of *Alice in Wonderland*, the one that explained the meanings behind the set pieces in the story. And she'd seen a display on him at the Science Museum in Oxford, where he had taught mathematics. In today's climate, she thought, he would likely be ostracized for spending so much time with a little girl. She liked him anyway.

This cathedral also had a library, and one could actually go inside. At first, she thought it looked like a museum. There were large cases with shiny silver goblets and plates, a whole collection. There were Elizabethan portraits high on the wood-paneled walls. But she could see that the books, closed behind glass doors, had identification tags on them, and were regularly used. As she walked along the shelves, she came upon an ordinary clothing rack hung with gowns and surplices. These were handy, and in use. Despite the tall medieval windows, this place was obviously alive.

～

Spring 1887

It was Wells' third year in London and he knew that he was losing his place in his own life.

Perhaps he felt too comfortable now. His arrival had not been auspicious. The single guinea from his coveted scholarship would not, he knew, allow for decent lodgings. His mother had an idea. An old friend of hers, who had unfortunately died, had a daughter who ran a boarding house in Westbourne Park. Sarah wrote and asked if there was a room for Bertie and received a positive response.

Wells knew that this place was not what his mother anticipated. Of the two couples, two boys, and two male lodgers, everyone was profligate. The women spent the days shopping and persuading strange men to buy them drinks and encouraged everyone to go out on the weekends. More than once Wells felt obligated to buy a round of drinks, and as a result had to go without lunch for a day or two. He got thinner, and more tired. Each day he walked from Westbourne Park across Kensington Gardens to get to the Normal School. It was well over two miles, and he had to hurry home in the evening before the Gardens closed and he couldn't pass through. On Sundays he was left with a young cousin who both encouraged and rejected his advances, and once his landlady made sexual overtures toward him in his bedroom. It was a very confusing place to try to study in the evenings. But of course he couldn't tell his mother.

His father Joseph had a niece, however, who worked in Kensington. She had been asked to keep an eye on young Herbert who was, after all, only eighteen. Wells told her about the boarding house, and she promptly arranged for a move to the home of Aunt Mary. Since she lived on Euston Road, this added another full mile to Wells' walk to college, but there was no rush in the evening since Hyde Park didn't close.

Aunt Mary's house had another source of appeal in cousin Isabel. She was kind and gentle and ladylike. Wells felt solid and grateful walking alongside her when she returned home from her work retouching photographs. There were lodgers in the house, and he often worked alone in his cold room, his clean underthings wrapped around his feet. But his distractions were not only at home. The first year had gone beautifully, because he had class with the great man himself, T. H. Huxley. Huxley was a brilliant lecturer, and Wells fell in love with zoology. While in his own mind he considered himself one of "Huxley's men," he never had the courage to speak to him. Once he held the door open for him and was too tongue-tied to say good morning. Another time, Huxley came around to his table in the laboratory, and his hands began to shake. But the great man just glanced at him and walked on by.

If only his other professors had been so awe-inspiring. But they weren't, and Wells instead had begun to abandon lectures and read more about politics and culture in the library. He became associated with the debate club and enjoyed the arguing so much he forgot to study. Geology was particularly dull, and by this point, he had begun failing his examinations. His scholarship would not be allowed to continue.

∽

It was when I lost my scholarship, said Wells, that I really began to deceive myself.

How so? said Katherine. It was not a good day, and she was drinking some tea.

I was a very confident young man, said Wells. I really thought I was awfully knowledgeable. I could talk about philosophy, and Malthus, and free love, and republicanism, and atheism. I talked about all these things to Isabel, and she seemed to listen. But she didn't really understand, and all my talk would overwhelm her. I thought maybe if she read Ruskin…

It doesn't sound like you were compatible, said Katherine. It also sounds like you were suffering from college sophomore syndrome, where you think you know everything but actually know very little.

I suppose so, said Wells. And somehow when I lost my scholarship I thought I'd be fine. I could do anything! I could write stories, I knew, because I'd gotten one published. I ignored the fact that the story was terrible. And I'd studied with Huxley, and read Plato, and I could walk in the park with this perfectly lovely if imperfect creature by my side. I would do great things, and be worthy of her, and be a great writer or something. And it somehow didn't seem important that I'd lost my scholarship, had no money, and possessed very few qualifications for getting a job.

That's how you ended up in Wales, said Katherine.

I thought Wales was a beautiful country, all green hills and lovely lakes. When the job opened at Holt Academy, I imagined a fine old school. The prospectus looked so promising.

Was it not a fine old school? asked Katherine.

Well, it was old. And dirty. And crowded. Boys slept two in a bed, with no one minding them. The food was poor, and there seemed to be no scheme or curriculum for the schoolwork. I actually had to teach scripture, a ridiculous idea, because many of them were studying to qualify for the Methodist clergy.

And it was only as I wrote to Simmons and to Elizabeth Healey (brilliant letters, I thought, as a man of letters would write) that I realized how desperate my situation had become. I had stupidly stepped away from my future as a fully qualified science teacher, thinking I'd be a teacher here anyway. But the job was poorly paid, as all my jobs would be now. I wrote and tried to consider myself a writer, then I'd look out on what they called the grounds and realized I was in hell. Who was I teaching, really, and why? Would anything I taught make any difference to boys just trying to pass a fairly simple clerical exam? What use would science be to them?

I know, said Katherine. That's the crux of teaching, qualified or not. How do you know what you're doing is important?

In my case, said Wells, it became clear that it wasn't, just about the time I got injured on the playing field.

Sometimes, said Katherine, it takes something awful and physical for you to find out you're in the wrong place in your life.

Katherine's love for Yorkshire created a cunning plan. Instead of the British Library main branch in London, she would travel to the Boston Spa branch. Most of the journals she ordered came from there anyway.

The library building was out on a road near, but not in, the town of Wetherby. Close enough, she thought. She referenced Google Maps, but it was hard to tell how long and difficult a walk it might be. And the bus, Bus 7, didn't seem to go there every day.

She had considered staying near the University of Sheffield or the University of Leeds, both of which had regular buses to the library. But those were only for staff and students. At her age it would be difficult to sneak on, and then she'd have to explain herself. She didn't like explaining herself.

So she stayed in Wetherby, in a rather expensive flat overlooking the river. She had lugged her suitcase along the pavement from the bus stop, rather than taking a taxi from Leeds. The flat was on two floors, and on the ground floor the traffic was loud out front, and the trees blocked the view of the river out back. The first evening, someone walked right along the windows to take out the rubbish.

But upstairs, the view of the river was unobstructed. The desk, however, was on the opposite side of the room from the river. She tugged it across the room, careful not to mar the floor. Underneath where the desk had been, unlike the tidiness of the rest of the flat, it was dirty, with dust and webs and a little girl's forgotten hair bow. She opened the windows to let in the evening breeze and sat down to try to write.

Then evening came. The first insect seemed inordinately large, with a fearsome black thorax and pointed translucent wings. Others followed: flies the size of airplanes, and a moth that seemed lost. The evening was spent guiding creatures back out the windows by waving magazines and standing on a chair.

The next day, Bus 7 was running to the library. Out of the flat, up the road past the garden (must stop in at some point), round the corner, past the new bar that had just closed, to the bus stand where a queue was forming. She kept her phone in front of her with the map, so she knew when to get off. Landing on a verge with no pavement and lots of grass next to the bus stand, she had to cross over to find somewhere to walk. Squeezing past rubbish bins (rubbish day was Wednesday, apparently) she found a semi-safe crossing for the road, went back to the other side, then up the smaller road to what looked like a toll booth.

Everything was clearly made for cars. The arrows on the road, the signs she couldn't quite make out, the toll booth. As she approached on foot, hoping no one would drive up behind her, Katherine saw a man in the booth, looking the other way. Pretending to be a vehicle, she squeezed past the barrier and approached the window.

The man looked taken aback. "Hullo," he said. He was wearing a jacket.

"I'm here to use the library?" she said uncertainly.

"Yes. All right. Follow the arrows on the pavement."

She looked around for pavement and saw only road.

"Over there," he said, pointing off to the left.

"Thank you," she said.

"Go right down that line till it turns green. Green means for walking to registration. It will take you to registration for the library. When you come back, just follow the green markers."

Going around the corner, she found the green marks on the pavement. It was all a little further than she'd planned to walk, across car parks. But the door was clearly marked, a proper glass door, and inside was a miniature version of the London British Library.

She had to go into a small room with small lockers, use the same plastic bags, put in a pound coin, and get a little key to keep with her. She was then inspected and passed into the Reading Room (only one) and found the main desk (only one).

Being clever, she had re-ordered books that she had used in London the week before, but she had not counted on there being a bank holiday in between. Most of the books had not arrived, and after searching on computers, the staff (only one) was most apologetic. In fact, they had only reserved two volumes, and only of *The University Correspondent*. Rather dejectedly (she had come a long way to be in a small institutional building at the end of a road not really in Yorkshire), she took her seat.

She had used these volumes before, but there was nothing for it but to look again. That's ok, she said to herself, I want to write an article some day on just this journal, which few people know about. I already have the articles by Wells according to the bibliography, so I'll look at the advertisements, the letters, the structure of the journal. And just in case (and because there's lots of time) I'll go page by page.

Twenty minutes later, she turned a page, rather listlessly really, and saw an article called "The Too-Ambitious Text-book." It was signed H. G. Wells. She looked again. She had already photographed an article called "The Use and Abuse of the Text-book," from a different journal, the year before. This wasn't that. She had been painstakingly collecting all of Wells' writings from his earlier life, all of those related to teaching science. Everything that came before *The Time Machine*. So what was this? Why hadn't she seen it?

It must be in the bibliographies, she thought, and took out her laptop. I don't have access to the printed ones, but the others are scanned and I can find them here.

After half an hour, she realized she had discovered an article that wasn't in any of the bibliographies. Her hands began to shake. She looked around, but there was no one to tell. How was this even possible, that this overly studied and massively published man, whose every pen-scratch was listed in bibliographies that were being printed while he was still in his prime years, wrote an unreprinted, unlisted article?

And yet there it was, discovered because she'd left a bug-ridden flat with a beautiful view of the river, gotten on a bus on the right day, crossed the road twice, followed the green markings through the carparks, then didn't obtain half of what she had ordered.

Wells wasn't there, of course. He'd never been to Yorkshire.

∽

Summer 1887

William Briggs' project was expanding, and so was his family.

"We need to move on and move up," he said to Ada. "I don't need this post anymore. The correspondence college is expanding. And you are run off your feet doing the work of both office clerk and mother."

Ada smiled. Little William Robinson was strong and healthy and was feeding well.

"What we need," said big William, "is a better name, and a better address. Oxford, or Cambridge." Knowing her husband, Ada began packing up the house.

Although he had attended neither Oxford nor Cambridge himself, Briggs was well aware of the cachet of those illustrious universities. He could situate his venture near one of them and use the address. Advertising was always foremost in his mind. He fixed on Cambridge. Realizing the potential for lawsuits if he actually used the name, he decided on University Correspondence College, with a Cambridge address.

First, he leased a building for offices, then later a larger building on the edge of Parker's Piece. He established not only correspondence courses by post, but a "residential" option in Cambridge itself. These would be attended by teachers at the school holidays.

"And you and baby William will be right here," he said. "We'll lease the whole terrace."

The venture was successful immediately. Short courses and longer courses were offered, studying for degree examinations in various subjects. This close to Cambridge University, there was no shortage of tutors happy to take on paid work. Maths and mechanics Briggs taught himself. He would write his own textbooks. Perhaps he should start his own press for publishing them.

Within a year, given the rise of demand for practical science, he began another venture. The University Tutorial College would offer science laboratories in London. A fifteen-minute walk from the University on Red Lion Square, these "practicals" would be taught by scholars in the various scientific subjects. So obviously he needed someone to teach biology.

∽

Whenever Katherine went north, and met people, they'd say, "But Wells is from the south, isn't he?" It was funny how everyone knew that, where he was from. To her knowledge, he'd never gone very far north at all.

I did, you know, he said, when I was recuperating. I stayed with the Burtons in Stoke-on-Trent.

That's not very far north, she said. I like Durham, myself.

∽

The Hemingway Coffee House was on the corner, Katherine knew, but it was hard to know where to park. She was nervous, and not sure why she had searched MeetUp for a writers' group. Her writing was non-fiction. Surely they would all be fiction writers.

She arrived anyway and was glad for the Writers Group sign on one of the tables. She had thought, how would one recognize a group of writers? Would they look frail and wan from not going outside? Behave gregariously because they rarely had human company? She sat at the table, and one by one introduced herself to each one, or they introduced themselves to her. Names were named, hands shaken.

"Now," said the leader, "my name is Alma, and I've been leading this group the last two years. We have some new writers here, so let's review the rules. I will introduce the topic, and then everyone will write for thirty minutes. You don't have to write on this topic if you don't want to. Some people are working on books already and just want time to add to their work. But you can use the theme if you wish. Now, critique. Once the thirty minutes are up, we each read our work. The rule is: no criticism. This is a friendly group. Okay?"

Everyone nodded and began to write. The topic was "I have a radio in my head." Katherine began to write on her laptop, and after a few sentences her thoughts of radio naturally turned to H. G. Wells. In 1938 his *War of the Worlds* had been presented on radio. When she was young she'd seen a TV movie about it. Orson Welles had set it in Grovers Mill, New Jersey, instead of Woking, Sussex. The legend was that Americans who tuned in late thought they were hearing a news report. They believed the Martians were really landing. They went crazy, packing their cars, grabbing the kids.

Except they didn't. The publicity said they did, and Orson Welles loved publicity, but it was like the hoax that had a hoax. So she wrote about that. Had to use her laptop to look up some dates. Typed fast. Ended right before 30 minutes.

Then they went around the table to read aloud. The man in the baseball cap and heavy jacket, heavy jowls, heavy eyelids, read slowly through the piece he'd written in pencil on a yellow legal pad. It was rambling and seemed to track his thinking about the universe and his own head. He interrupted himself frequently with, "well, that's what I was thinking, anyway." Then he looked around. Katherine, remembering "no criticism," stayed silent.

The young, bearded man across the table said, "I really liked the way you detailed your own thoughts. Very real."

The bird-eyed woman with dyed hair said, "That's true. It seemed very real. Do you really think about all that stuff?"

"Yeah, I do," he said, pleased. He puffed up a bit.

Alma said, "What I really liked was the way you used the word 'hope.'" He nodded. Katherine wasn't sure what to say. She thought she was following the rules and they weren't. After the bird-eyed woman started to read her own piece, she realized she had been supposed to say something nice. No criticism must mean not saying anything negative. It didn't mean no comment.

As the others read, she made sure to say something encouraging each time. Then it was her turn. She started reading, and about half-way through realized she'd written far more than any of the others. But she kept going till the end. There was a silence.

"Wow," said the big-jacketed man, "you wrote all that just now?"

"Yes," said Katherine.

"How did you know all that stuff?" said the young bearded man.

"Most I know," she said, "but I just looked up the dates real quick."

"Hmmm," said Alma.

She went back for the next four weeks. Each time, she thought, I'll write a different style. Less factual, more fiction. One week she wrote a children's story, one week a parable, one week a poem. All of them were much longer than anyone else's. She began to get embarrassed. She was competing with herself, trying new things. But she realized that from the outside, it might look like she was competing with them. After Christmas, she didn't return.

❧

At home, Katherine had put up pictures of the Yorkshire Dales. They made her feel better, because she always felt better when she was there. Garsdale was her favorite.

Shall I tell you about when I was ill? he said.

Which time? she said. She was lying in bed, one of those days where she was so sore it was hard to stay lying down, and just as hard to get up and do her stretches. One of those days when death kept reminding her there were more appointments coming up.

When I got injured in Wales, said Wells, playing with those horrible boys at Holt Academy. What a miserable place. I think that idiot did it on purpose, fouling me right in the kidneys.

Then the doctor said I had consumption. I went from urinating blood to coughing it up. I was quite sure I was going to die, and the doctor thought so too. I didn't want to die, when I hadn't done anything yet. I wanted to be remembered. And it annoyed me to no end that I was still a virgin. I was taken to Uppark, where Doctor Collins put ice on my chest. I wrote a lot of letters to people, thinking they were my last.

I'm not writing letters, she said. I'm writing about you.

But I began writing other things, stories and verses, he said, like I had as a boy. I hadn't done much when I was studying for exams. Now I had time to read, especially poetry and novels. Writing fiction started to seem like something I wanted to do. I kept that desire after I got better.

She looked out the window. Fall was coming, and the sunlight entered at an odd angle, with the color that made her wonder about wildfires. She had written things, all her life. Stories, poems, diaries. Most hadn't been read by anyone. A few poems in the college magazine, a few articles in an online teaching journal. After much work, one article had finally been published about H. G. Wells. But nothing big, no books or novels.

You, she said, were twenty-one. I am fifty-six.

☙

Portland Place. The building was hard to find. The Anaesthesia Heritage Center? The Anaesthesia Museum. There it was. "The Association of Anaesthetists of Great Britain and Ireland" was the bigger sign, the museum sign smaller and below it. She went inside. The foyer was nicely laid out, with palms and columns. Quite grand, really, considering its size. At the end of the foyer was a desk. Important-looking people were walking about. But no one was at the desk. She stood and waited.

Finally one of the young men scurrying about reluctantly took notice of her.

"Can I help you?" he said.

"Yes, please. I'm here to see the museum."

He looked puzzled, as if this was a request that occurred only on an annual basis.

"Ah," he said, "I'll see if I can get someone to help you," and scurried off.

A minute later, another man entered from a door in the hall behind the desk. He looked like he belonged at the desk.

"May I help you?" he said, pleasantly. Bedside manner, she thought.

"Yes, please. I'm here to see the museum."

"Ah," he said. He looked down at the appointment book, then seemed to realize that was foolish. But it was too late.

"Have you an appointment?" he asked.

"No," she said. "I'm sorry. I didn't know I needed one. I'm only here today." She had found that it was good to indicate that her time was short when she didn't want to be asked to return later. He frowned, then, realizing he was frowning, smiled faintly.

"Let me get the key," he said, "and I'll take you down there."

A museum in the basement, she thought. Intriguing.

He returned with the key. "This way," he said, and went through a side opening toward a narrow flight of stairs. Katherine followed him down.

"Here we are," he said, and turned to leave, then seemed to realize he should say something. "The museum is in these rooms," he said, motioning to the area. "You'll find equipment, and a library, and all the information you need on the signs." Since this might have sounded abrupt, he added, "I'll be upstairs if you need anything."

"Is it all right for me to be down here for a while?" she asked. "I'd like to take my time."

"Of course," he said. "Take all the time you like."

Someone had gone to a lot of work in the small space. There were pictures and information on all the walls, a screen showing a video, and cases squeezed together displaying anesthetic equipment. She knew a little about it, because her father had been an anesthesiologist (the American term). He'd practiced here in Britain for a time, so she went first to that cabinet to get a feel for the technology of the 1960s. Then she worked backward in time, to the cotton masks of the Victorian era, the comparisons of chloroform and ether, the designs of the breathing apparatus. Drawers pulled open to show more equipment, which were all clearly labeled and dated. She noted, not surprisingly, that the techniques seemed to advance more quickly during wartime.

One of the rooms was a library, but she had a feeling she wasn't supposed to touch anything. It looked like a working library, even if it was in the basement museum. The video was more about the professional association than the museum, so she didn't watch long. It began to feel strange to be the only person there. She went up to the desk to thank the man who'd helped her. But he was gone, and other men in suits were scurrying about doing important things. She let herself out.

∽

She was in the chair in her bedroom, with the heat pad, reading Susan Sontag.

Did you know, she said, that Sontag equated cancer with consumption?

No, said Wells. But why is that relevant?

Just listen, she said. In *Illness as Metaphor*, she said that tuberculosis was seen as a passionate, creative disease. Almost trendy. Like in *La Traviata*, or *La Boheme*, or *Camille*. It's a disease of those who are artistic, who are too fragile to survive the fire of their own genius. Like Keats.

It's true, said Wells. When they thought I had consumption, I tried to act the part. People were sympathetic. That sympathy meant I could return to Uppark, even though the upstairs folks were tired of us boys hanging around.

Katherine went on. Cancer, said Sontag, is seen now as being about repressed feelings and creativity. Things that aren't being released that should be. But it was seen differently by doctors in other times.

The problem with associating such patterns with illness, said Wells, is that it might make people feel that their illness is their own fault.

That, said Katherine, is what Sontag said too.

When really it's about doctors not knowing what to do, he said.

There are some things doctors do very well, said Katherine. Like anesthesia.

6

Katherine arrived in Cambridge for the first time by train. Using UniversityRooms.com, she had arranged to stay at St. Catherine's College. Then, and every time since, she always seemed to be there for Open Days, when parents and their children came to look at the college. She would become accustomed to people walking across the grass and peering in her ground floor window, where her instant cocoa packets were arrayed on the ledge.

Unlike Oxford's Bodleian, Cambridge University Library was in an enormous modern building that looked like a coal-fired power plant. To get there, one had to walk quite a distance across the Backs, then down a rather residential-looking path. The library was very clean, the books lined up like soldiers on regimented shelves. The doors were glass, and the tea room very quiet.

The glass-doored Reading Room contained some records from the College of Preceptors, who gave examinations for teaching and supervised subjects taught in middle-class schools in the 19th century. Wells had taken some of these exams as a boy, because his mother wanted him to be a shop clerk.

Katherine went up to the desk, where a librarian who obviously had better things to do didn't look her way. The method here was to fill out a slip and put it in a box, then take a seat. The items would be brought to you rather than being collected at the desk. You knew this because there were vast sets of laminated instructions taped to the librarian's counter. She chose a desk near the counter so the staff wouldn't have to walk too far.

The librarian arrived and placed the books before her, saying not a word. Most were modern records, not of much use. But as she went back through the volumes she discovered lists of members of the College of Preceptors. Membership had various levels, and she found the name of J. V. Milne, for whom Wells had worked at Henley House School. This wasn't surprising, as he had been known as an educationalist. But the name of Thomas Morley did surprise her. He had run the commercial academy Wells had attended in Bromley, and the school did not come out well in Wells' autobiography or later writings.

So she began looking back through the examination lists, and was pleased to find Wells' name among them, since these records went back so far. But then she came upon the texts of the examinations themselves, and found the bookkeeping examination for the college, only a few years after Wells had been there.

"I wonder," she asked the librarian, "whether I could get the records for a few years before this?"

The librarian was a young man with oily dark hair, possibly a university student. Rather than trying for a helpful expression, his sallow face displayed only exaggerated patience. It was clear he'd rather not be hunting down orders that were beyond that which had been originally requested using the slips and the box.

"We can try," he said. The "we" was strange — there was no one else behind the desk. Perhaps, she thought, there are minions in the stacks. "Just fill out the forms."

She filled out more forms, one for each possible volume. He looked at them. "We'll need the exact information here, here, and here," he said, pointing to the various lines. She added in the full titles (knowing there were no other similar titles) and the dates (knowing that the volume numbers were the dates).

"Put it there," he said. She put it there.

Waiting at her desk, she could just see the reference counter. She looked through the book she had for the third time, took a few notes, and waited. After about twenty minutes, the librarian slowly got up, and removed the small stack of slips from the box. All of them were Katherine's. He went very slowly to an area approximately ten feet from the box and pulled three volumes off a nearby shelf. She could see him through the glass.

Rather inconvenient, glass. Surely if there had been real walls he would have been able to conceal the fact that the volumes were so close and easy to find. Obviously there was no need for minions.

Another young man came through the glass doors, from another reading room across the way. He put the books down as he chatted with his colleague about, she overheard, nothing of particular import. After he left, the librarian picked up her books again. Depositing the volumes on her desk, he brusquely pulled the slips out of them to retain, gave a little snort, and returned to the counter.

Third volume, and there it was. The date was right, the subject was right. This would have been the exact bookkeeping test that Wells would have taken as a child. She was so excited she photographed all the pages, then bounced up to the desk.

"Thank you," she said. "Do you realize that this book has the exact bookkeeping examination that H.G. Wells took as a child?"

"Does it," he said.

"Yes! I'm very excited to see this."

"Yes," he said. There was no glimmer of interest at all. She thought, perhaps people make discoveries like this all the time, and he's accustomed to the excitement of researchers on topics about which he cares not at all. It must be quite tedious for him.

༄

Summer 1888

The studio was tiny, and Wells had to share it with Cole. But he wanted to do a good job for Jennings, drawing out the diagrams to use for his teaching. Sometimes he would copy them in the British Library Reading Room, but the light was better here.

Cole, though, often blocked the window, ruining the light. He needed the window light for his own project. He was a microtomist, making slides for schools to purchase. The room was filled with various jars of specimens: jellyfish, a cat's toe, human hair. Wells tried to act like an old scientist, surrounded by the usual natural objects. But his mind would think up stories, because he knew others would find many of the specimens creepy. There were even some human samples, including part of an old woman's hand in a jar. Cole wouldn't say where he got it.

Jennings couldn't pay Wells a lot to draw diagrams, but it was more than he'd had before. Ever since that day when the ha'penny in his pocket turned out to be a discolored shilling, he'd realized how close he had been to starvation. He'd come to London before to make his way, but he'd failed, multiple times. Well, he wouldn't fail Jennings. He had been a true friend to give H. G. this task, even though he wasn't the best at drawing. He'd make Jennings proud.

But what Cole created was more like art. Thin slivers of material, sliced carefully with his steady hands. Mounted on a slide, with special paper labels that looked like fine printing. Separated by felt in beautiful wooden boxes, the slides were sold in sets. Someday, thought Wells, they will be recognized for what they are. Someday, people will pay a lot to have these sets, and display them in the parlor to show friends they have taste and style. Not my drawings, he thought. Someday, I'll be having someone do my drawings so I can just write.

❧

Katherine had an appointment with the archivist at the University of London. Harriet Green had replied to Katherine's query by inviting her to look through an old file cabinet that had been there for years. They might have papers referring to Briggs' London operation in Red Lion Square, or they might not. Katherine was welcome to take a look.

It was a sweltering day in June. Although she had stayed nearby in Bloomsbury, the walk to the archive was oppressive. Inside the building it wasn't much better. She had expected an older building, but it looked like it had been built in the 1980s or 90s, a low-slung modern place with an old-fashioned sign that looked fairly recent. It had two floors of files and boxes, and a corner room at the back where the staff took tea.

The file cabinet was near a window. All the windows were opened, but the air didn't move. There was a man there, in blue jeans, pushing around a large portable air-conditioner, trying to get its hose to go out the window. He pressed a button, and a low roar issued from the machine. He smiled at Katherine.

"Thank you," said Katherine. "That's helpful." He then closed all the windows and left. It had not seemed possible for the room to be more airless. But it was.

Katherine set up at one of the small oak tables, careful to move her water bottle far from her work area. She had always been aware of her own clumsiness. From difficulty riding a bike, to the impossibility of roller skates, to pepperoni landing in her lap on a first date, her own inability to work gracefully in space had been proven many times. Trust her to be looking at 19th century papers, and spill water all over them.

Katherine began going through the file cabinet, which contained mostly twentieth century documents. A lot of meeting minutes, going back to the 1940s. They made interesting reading ("Mr. Smithson was unable to attend as he was due at the War Office") but there was nothing about Wells or the University Correspondence College run by William Briggs. Nothing went back far enough. She had planned to spend several hours, and it had taken less than thirty minutes to discover there was nothing there.

This was a problem. Harriet had made special arrangements for her to access the cabinet. She couldn't just say, "oops, nothing here" and leave. Plus the archivist had invited her to lunch. So in her awkwardness, Katherine stayed through the morning, going over documents of little interest, taking useless notes. The room became warmer and warmer. She got up and opened windows, fully aware of the environmental implications of doing so with the air conditioner running full blast.

This was not her first English heat wave. It seemed that each summer they had one. And each year everyone talked about how novel it was, which made no sense. Centuries of chilly summers had made it impossible to believe that each summer now had weeks of unbearable heat. It was clearly the new normal, yet everyone was surprised. The streets were hot. Katherine often found herself crossing to the shady side of the street just to go a few blocks in London. One year she'd had to go shopping because her feet kept swelling unpleasantly in the overly warm weather. She'd been forced to buy elastic sandals for £5 at Primark and had never been more grateful for a pair of ill-fitting shoes in her life.

By the time Harriet came to collect her for lunch, she had finished drinking all her water and the useless files had been carefully replaced.

"Anything useful?" asked Harriet.

"Oh, yes indeed," Katherine lied. "I found everything I need and am quite ready for lunch."

"I know just the place," said Harriet. "Are you okay with walking?"

Katherine had not yet learned the walking code. She assumed, in this heat, perhaps a few blocks. In fact, she had seen a collection of restaurants just down the road. It was only as they passed these, Harriet moving briskly, that she realized her mistake. She gamely kept up, one block, then two, then three, then further through Bloomsbury ("this really is the intellectual heart of London") then beyond. Calthorpe Street crossed Grays Inn Road and became Guilford Street. This makes the distance seem even longer, thought Katherine. In California, streets go on for miles with the same name. El Camino Real practically ran the length of the state, although there were breaks. A bus passed, radiating its heat up onto the pavement. Just as Katherine was ready to beg for mercy, they stopped at a gloriously ornate terra cotta building facing Russell Square.

The restaurant, unfortunately, was very nice, with glass inlaid doors and red decorous carpet. The lobby where one waits was separated from the dining room by a decorative wall. They were seated quickly, mirrors and potted palms all around. But Katherine was breathless and sweating and simply out of place here in such a condition. When they asked the waiter for water, Harriet seemed to suddenly realize that Katherine was exhausted. Americans, she thought. They seem so fit, but they aren't.

Brits, thought Katherine. They look so ordinary, but they're really quite fit and can walk for miles. This is how they survived the Japanese-led Death March during the war.

~

I liked my job at Henley House School, said Wells. J. V. Milne was a wonderful man who cared very much about teaching.

I do care, said Katherine, but sometimes it's hard. She was resting.

When I first arrived, said Wells, he gave me money and told me to buy equipment. The previous science master had blown everything up.

How? asked Katherine.

He mixed a powerful potion, too powerful for the cheap glassware. When it broke he used the other glassware to help, and it broke too. The cupboard was full of broken glassware. I didn't realize until I lifted up a flask, and it neatly detached from its base. Even the balance wasn't useful, because the weights were missing.

So I convinced Milne that me drawing on the blackboard with colored chalk would be a much better option. I made a sound pedagogical argument, about the role of demonstration and the vagaries of experimentation. Experimentation, I said, could be unpredictable, even dangerous. And with demonstration, I could teach them to draw, a crucial skill for doing science. I was, after all, the science master.

Milne was relieved, I could tell, said Wells. It would also be far less expensive. He was less certain about me demonstrating dissection, however. Worried about parental complaints, the horror and the gore. I promised to do them underwater, cleanly, and draw everything on the blackboard. He agreed.

I believe, said Katherine adjusting gently for the pain, you got to write there too?

Yes, the *Henley House School Magazine*.

I had a hard time finding that, she said. There aren't many copies around now. Almost as bad as the *Science Schools Journal*, from when you were at South Kensington.

That, Wells said, is entirely my fault. I bought up and destroyed as many copies as I could find. The writing was terrible. So, the *Magazine*. It gave me the chance to both write out some science principles, and to have some fun with my pupils. I wrote a column once all about their summer interests, using their initials. They really enjoyed that. Kept jostling each other, saying oh, that's you. He's talking about you!

I also got to take them on field trips. All boys, you know — boys' school. I took them to the zoo. Milne's youngest, little Alan, went along too. I tried to teach them some zoology, but it was just such a nice day to be out of the school. Little Alan was quite enchanted by the bear, as I recall.

Yes, said Katherine. He did something with that, later on.

~

She'd arrived at the conference a day early, so it would be a good time to scope out the room. As she made her way downstairs, she saw a tall man in a tweed suit. Professor Marks was talking to the students at the registration table, taking his badge and struggling to pin it to his lapel.

"Hello, Professor," she said, smiling broadly.

"Katherine!" said Professor Marks. "I didn't know you'd be here."

She tried not to gush. He had been her mentor so long ago, her defender, her knight in shining armor.

"Yes," she said proudly. "I organized a panel, so I've come to get a program so I can see where we'll be."

She was tempted to go on about the panel, but knew that around Professor Marks she tended to act like a child hoping for daddy's approval. So instead she said, "I'm so glad to see you."

He smiled, and his eyes crinkled. He had such a kind face. You'd never guess the force of will behind it.

"How long has it been since we worked together?" he said.

That he even thought of it as working together made her very happy. She had helped write a workbook for the students, and was his teaching assistant, but he'd been far more to her.

"I think," she said, wondering whether to mention what he'd done for her, and then realizing she couldn't not mention it, "back when you convinced the other faculty to keep me on, even though I couldn't do a PhD. That would be almost twenty-five years ago."

"And now you teach community college, am I right?"

Thinking back to her graduate school days, she had not planned to teach community college. She remembered the one student there who taught at one. The others ignored him. She remembered him going in and out of the teaching assistant room, silently, with his brown briefcase.

"Yes, it's a wonderful job," she said, "and I wouldn't have gotten it without you letting me stay as your teaching assistant. I'd have had to quit."

"Oh, yes, I remember," he said. "But you had such good ideas, and were so determined, and it just didn't seem right to take your job away." He glanced at his watch. "I'm sorry, but

I'm due at a committee meeting," he said. "I do hope to see you at your session."

She shook his hand. It seemed silly, but she just needed another way to thank him.

Giving her name at the table, Katherine received the program. Their panel was on the very last session of Sunday, the very last day. That didn't seem very nice. Maybe she just didn't know enough people in the organization to get a better slot. The panel had been assigned the Windward Suite. She walked across the reception area, and began looking at the names on the ballroom doors. Aloha Suite, Kona Ballroom. This place had a thing about Hawai'i. No Windward Suite.

She took the escalator to the next floor up, where the smaller rooms were. Maui, Kauai, Reef. There was a passageway to the other side of the floor. On the sign pointing to the passageway was "Restrooms" and "Telephone." That couldn't be right. She went around the other way to the other rooms: Kontiki, Molokai, Leeward. Surely Windward was near? She peeked down the passageway toward the restrooms and telephone, and there it was. In the middle of the passage. An indented door with the letters in gold: Windward Suite. It was behind the women's toilets.

For the next two days, Katherine attended sessions. She tried to go to the Victorian ones, but there weren't many options. Sitting through yet another paper where the British Empire was the evil-doer in need of penance and redemption, she became frustrated and attended sessions on the 18th century, enjoying the rationalism. Then it was Sunday. She got up too early, nervous, and packed up. She put on her presentation clothes. But where was the blazer? She'd brought the blazer, surely. But it wasn't there. She'd lost it, or forgotten it. Her blouse wasn't suitable on its own. All she had was the pale blue cardigan she'd travelled in. It was a bit rumpled and smelled of airplane.

Katherine turned on the shower very hot, hung up the sweater in the bathroom, went out and closed the door. The steam should help. But the fact was, it was a cardigan, not a blazer. Even with her nice scarf, she would look like someone's grandmother rather than a scholar. And there was nothing to be done. She sprayed it with her lavender perfume.

She got to the room early. As the panel organizer, she wanted to be sure there were glasses of water. Attendees were leaving sessions in the other rooms. She crossed a line of people heading to the restrooms. She set up, sat down at the panel table, and waited.

Reggie showed up first, his red hair a little frazzled but his suit impeccable. He was from a Canadian university, but they had no real department there. So he behaved more like an independent scholar. His paper was about Victorian medicine in Quebec. Sandra arrived next, looking calm and collected, which Katherine knew was an act. Sandra had great confidence in herself but was pulled in many directions by work and family. She was wearing a black blazer, crisp and pressed.

"I lost my blazer," said Katherine in an undertone as Sandra sat next to her. "I look like a grandmother."

"You look like a very lovely grandmother," said Sandra.

The moderator came in, a graduate student who was delighted to play hostess. She shook everyone's hand and sat down with her portfolio in front of her, tugging her pert and professional blazer down a bit as she sat. Two conference-goers came in the door, looked around, and went back out. A woman in all black, with very short dyed purple hair and a piercing in her nose, came in and took a seat in the third row, smiling at the panel. It was almost time to start, according to the program. A young male scholar came in, and slouched into a seat at the back. Sandra's husband Rick came in, waved, and took a seat at the side. That was it. Three people. There were more than that on the panel.

Katherine looked at her paper and began to introduce the others.

~

I get so excited about teaching history, said Katherine. Every term I'm so enthusiastic to get started. I think I've solved all the problems from the previous term, and that this time it will be the best ever. They'll learn that history is the context of everything.

It was not a good day. Class had gone well, because she had the energy to give a lecture with many interesting asides. The students had smiled and nodded. But as usual, they had taken few notes. I don't quiz enough, she reminded herself. That's because I don't want to grade quizzes. Now that class was over, she was tired again. Coming home, she'd taken a hot shower. She then bundled up in one of her collection of "ratty old sweaters," as her friend Patty called them. The chair beckoned, and the laptop. She began planning next term, not knowing whether there would be one.

For me it was science teaching, said Wells. I know later they'll say I was a writer, like it was destiny. A writer of fiction, then a social critic. But I wrote dozens of articles on science teaching. Not just because I had taught science myself, but because I really believed it could change everything.

To me, Wells continued, the issue was between science as a collection of facts, and scientific thinking. The purpose of science teaching is to engender a scientific habit of thought. One could easily fill up pupils with scientific facts, and not only bore them, but prevent them seeing the larger picture, the reason for science, and the reasoning behind science.

Perhaps it doesn't matter, said Katherine, what the subject is?

Oh, but it does, said Wells. It matters very much. That's why I was against the infernal habit of teaching classical languages. Would it be more useful to habits of mind to learn Greek, or to learn science? It would be fine, I suppose, if there were fewer subjects all together. But there were so many subjects occupying the school years.

Nowadays, said Katherine, there are many subjects also. But the primary subjects are English, mathematics, social science, and science. Art is left till last.

The timetable, said Wells, is overcrowded. Add to your subjects bookkeeping, metallurgy, shorthand, drawing, commercial geography, mechanics, chemistry. I understand chemistry, of course, but memorizing the elements does not inspire scientific thinking. If we focused instead on instilling habits of mind, the leaders of the future would be sound, analytical thinkers. Knowledge would expand. Sense would be seen.

He was getting insistent, and his voice was getting higher. Is that why you joined the socialists? asked Katherine.

The socialists were the only ones looking at society rationally, he said. And I did join the Fabians, although their middle-class outlook drove me to abandon them. It was difficult to talk to people who wanted to look after those who were poor but had never been poor themselves.

It's interesting, she said, that you will go on to write fiction, then polemical works, then a history of the world. Everyone assumes my interest in you was because you wrote history. But to you, I think, that was a sideline because you wanted a clear, rational history that told a story.

I did believe in the power of narrative, Wells said. I started writing fiction, but there was always an important moral to each tale. But as I kept going, it seemed like people just enjoyed the story. They didn't learn from the moral. I think perhaps I was always a journalist, never a novelist. So, when they didn't understand, I had to start telling them, straight out.

That wasn't as much fun, said Katherine. It's been my problem too. Students want stories, the stories of history. They don't want to study and learn the patterns, the way history reveals humanity. They just want a rousing good tale. So, when that happens, I too start telling them straight out.

And it isn't as much fun, said Wells.

No, it isn't, said Katherine. One could, of course, use the form of dialogue to make such points.

One could indeed, said Wells.

71

7

The train had arrived at Durham, but Katherine had never been there. It was in the evening and beginning to get dark.

Safety, of course, was a concern to any traveler. Women, she'd been told, were especially likely targets. With her recent deformity and her age, she worried less about sexual attack. With her discount clothing and $85 suitcase, she worried less about robbery. But crazy people could be anywhere, so she usually tried to look like she knew where she was going.

Her confident walk had been noted before. After her introduction to chat rooms, and the advent of online teaching, and Learning Management Systems, it seemed that the web was a whole world. Second Life was a virtual world, and some professors were trying to use it for education. She duly created a character. But where some users created fantasy characters, she wanted her avatar to look like her. So while foxes with hats and flying fairy princesses filled the virtual lecture halls, she had an avatar that any of her real-life colleagues would recognize.

But she couldn't get the walk right. The female avatar tended to have a rather ladylike walk. In the end, she acquired a "walk" through the virtual marketplace and applied it to her character. The one that worked best was called Power Walk. It was a shame, because you had to hold down a key every time the avatar walked anywhere.

Virtual worlds were not something Katherine was good at. She knew her attitude was all wrong. With no interest in fantasy, or drunken schmoozing, there weren't many spaces that were comfortable. And then there was the technology. She had never been a gamer. The keyboard was awkward and the controls complicated. She'd tried to practice the basics of crossing a virtual room and sitting down. But her avatar invariably got stuck in a chair, the body bits entangled with the chair bits. It was embarrassing. She'd rudely walk through walls to enter a room, accidentally bump into other avatars, get trapped on the bottom of the pool. Humiliation, she decided, took up quite enough time in the real world. There was no need to experience it online.

Katherine used her real-life power walk to head down the train platform. Durham was not, she knew, a large station. And yet she was almost immediately lost. Either way around the building, there did not seem to be anywhere to catch a taxi. She knew from the maps it was too far to walk with her bags, and that there was a large hill downward into town.

Coming back through the station for a third time, she found herself in the car park. She spotted her seat partner, a man she'd conversed with briefly on the train. The topic had been sports. An important World Cup game had been going on, and groups had been variously cheering or booing as they watched on their devices. She and the man had poked fun at these football fanatics, assured that there were more important things in the world. He was now heading toward a car. She caught up with him.

"Hello again," she said breathlessly, dragging her bag over the bumpy surface. He was putting his bag in the boot.

"Hello!" he said.

"Do you happen to know where I can catch a taxi into town?"

He looked around. She felt a little better as it became obvious he didn't either. Maybe the place was confusing after all.

"I don't," he said. "Would you like a lift somewhere? I'm going in to town."

So here it was. Safety. Getting late. She was tired. He was a stranger, or at best a brief acquaintance. He smiled politely.

The thing is, she thought, I know it doesn't matter that he seems nice. Some axe murderers, she was sure, seemed nice. She had watched many British mysteries over the years. On her own, in a strange town, she knew it broke every rule she had taught to other women over the years.

"Would you mind?" she said. "I don't know the town and I need to go to Neville Street."

"Well I don't know where Neville Street is," he said, "but the SatNav will."

It didn't, but he found it anyway. Some people, she thought, are just incredibly kind.

∽

Katherine stood at the front of the classroom, and for once it was full of professors instead of college students.

What's important, she explained, is that your teaching take precedence over the technology. Teaching over the internet should not be about the technology. It's always about teaching and learning.

She had the professors assess their own strengths and weaknesses in teaching, and then guided the workshop into how to make these a reality in the online environment. Later, she would make herself available for webinars, and she invited guests who were experts in educational technology to help her teach faculty. She did it for years, and was never paid for it.

Why, asked Wells, would you teach without getting paid?

Money, said Katherine, means power. If I had allowed them to pay me, they would have had control over the process, and determined how everyone taught.

Still, said Wells, you must be paid enough in your regular teaching to spare the time.

I am, she said.

This internet, this web, he said, it seems very similar to a World Brain, a library for everyone, with potentially all the knowledge of the world in it.

It is sort of like that, only tainted with what you'd expect of human beings — their foibles, prejudices, and hatred. But you saw the potential of such a thing, for learning.

It also looks, he said, like what I did, tutoring students by post to prepare them for the examinations. Only the delay is much shorter.

Yes, she said, it's mere seconds now.

Do you, he asked, do your marking at home, or in the park, or in chop shops, like I did?

I do indeed. And even while traveling, to meet you.

⌇

The second time Katherine went to Durham she was more aware that there was no reason to be there, or at least none related to her research She also didn't know the town, and became lost trying to find Crook Hall, where she had heard there were lovely gardens, a little house, and a tea room.

The sun was hot. She walked through the cool house, admiring the books on the shelves and the furniture in the rooms. The gardens were lovely, with so many flowers that simply didn't exist in California, and little twining paths where you'd turn a corner and bump into another visitor.

The girl at the tea shop brought the pot, then asked where she was from. California, said Katherine. I've seen you, said the girl. You're the one who walks around town in your red coat. Katherine laughed.

She asked why Katherine was in England, so she explained about her project. The girl asked whether Wells had any connection to Durham.

"Not at all," said Katherine. "He never went north."

The girl raised an eyebrow.

"In fact," Katherine said, "I don't know why I feel drawn to come back here. It has nothing to do with my research. I just love the place so much — I have no idea why. Maybe it's the cathedral, with its Norman architecture, and the tomb of St. Cuthbert."

St. Cuthbert was not a saint she knew about before she came to Durham. She had learned about him at a conference here at the university, a conference intended for graduate students. She had been by far the oldest person there, the only American, and had felt terribly awkward just attending to listen. History conferences in the States were large affairs, where one could hide. This one was just a few dozen people, and they were all too polite to ask why on earth she was there.

But one afternoon, there was a walking tour of the city for those attending the conference from elsewhere. Quite sure she qualified, she joined the tour. The guide, a historian, seemed bored as he told the tales of Durham. She learned about St. Cuthbert, whose body was carried here from Lindisfarne. Apparently the dun cow that came with the monks had refused to go further, and they had decided that meant the saint wanted to stay.

The walk continued, quite long really, past the Bryson Library. By then Katherine knew that when an English person said a short walk, miles were often involved. English walks tired her, because although she loved walking, she wasn't used to it. And her body just didn't want to do long treks of any kind anymore.

She felt sorry for their guide, because no one walking seemed that interested, or wanted to engage in the history. So she began to walk beside instead of behind him, and asked questions.

"I noticed," she said, "that the aspect of the city seems to face away from the river. Why is that?"

The historian's face immediately lightened at the question, and he became animated explaining about the defensive arrangements, the cut of the river, the need for possible escape at the head of the peninsula. The rest of the afternoon was much brighter.

When she first visited the cathedral, she'd felt very much at home. As a non-Christian historian, this felt only half-way odd.

The proportions of the place, humanistically scaled like a Renaissance church but centuries older, impressed upon her a peace and solemnity she'd rarely felt. She went behind the altar, climbing the crooked stone steps with the iron handrail to a raised area at the back. When she sat next to the tomb of Cuthbert, she sensed the calm, mellow heart of the cathedral. She sat, waited, said nothing, thought only of the place she was in. A canon entered as if on a stage, accompanied by people dressed in bright African clothes. Behind them came men in severe business suits, obviously security of some kind.

The canon spoke to the illustrious visitors. This place, he said, is very special. His guests walked carefully around the brass plate with Cuthbert's name, the "u" shaped like a "v." They looked at the tall candlesticks, the embroidered pillows for kneeling, the iron boxes for donations with candles all around for lighting. They looked up at the modern painting but did not sit on the benches around the edge of the space.

"People come here," said the canon, "even people who are not religious. Even people who do not believe in God. They come here, and they feel something. Something very special."

The visitors nodded, and the group silently walked down the stairs on the opposite side.

I feel it, she thought. I feel that something special.

Katherine now walked across Palace Green, heading toward the cathedral.

It's unfortunate, thought Katherine. You'd think H. G. Wells would have some kind of connection to the north, but he just doesn't. I have no reason to be here. I guess Durham is just for me, like a holiday from my research holiday.

Then she looked up, and in front of the Palace Green Library was a sign. "Time Machines: The Past, The Future, and How Stories Take Us There."

She went in. The walls had quotations by H. G. Wells. There under glass was the manuscript of *The Time Machine*, in Wells' handwriting. Katherine stared at the many cross-outs and changed words and felt so much better about her own work.

He did it too, she thought. Never satisfied. Always trying to improve things.

～

Surely, said Wells, it should be easy to find the things I wrote.

It isn't, said Katherine. Your science teaching writings, for example, are scattered all over the place. Different journals, different libraries.

Still, he said.

It's more than that, said Katherine. You made a lot of references that people wouldn't understand. I couldn't just put your stuff out there. You dropped names. In one article, you referenced Miall, Todd, and Murché. I had no idea who these people were. And I had to find out, or no one would understand now what you meant.

Did you find them? he said.

I did, using the internet, your World Brain, she said. Miall was Moses Miall. I had to search for Miall, then narrow down the era, then find something to do with teaching. I was able to find a scanned copy of his *Practical Remarks on Education* from 1822. You liked him because he advocated personal attention to individual students, considering their ability. Murché isn't a common name either, so I was able to find out that he was Vincent T. Murché, who published two science readers for children in 1895. But Todd was much harder.

Because his name was so common, said Wells.

Exactly. So it was all about search terms. Todd + educationalist. Todd + nineteenth century. Todd + nineteenth century + schoolmaster. Have you any idea how many schoolmasters were named Todd? There were several in England, and one in Australia. I kept going down the wrong rabbit holes. And when I found David P. Todd, at first I thought you couldn't mean him because he was American. But in one article, you mentioned a magazine that I knew was *Scientific American*, so you must have known American scientists. I finally discovered that David P. Todd was not only at

78

Amherst Observatory, he also wrote a manual on the eclipse of the sun. It contained good drawings and instructions on how to view it. That's how I knew you meant him.

And you did all that without a library? he asked.

It is a library. It's a very big library, at my fingertips. But not everything is there.

～

Katherine returned her eyes to the phone's screen to read *The Island of Doctor Moreau*. There was no point looking up at the counter, crowded with patients signing in for their tests. There was a line at the reception area on the left. She had stood in that line, patiently, wondering how she kept from screaming. No one in line was screaming, and for a second she wondered why. How could people stand in line like this, and act as if this were a normal thing? They focused on the paperwork. She couldn't give a damn about the paperwork.

Reading on her phone wasn't enjoyable. For many literate readers, the internet craze had settled into one invention. The electronic reader, the Kindle, had captured the imagination. One could download many books and carry them all with you. But backlit reading was what Katherine did most of the time, teaching online. To read for herself was to relax. A screen was too much like work. And books, the tangible, paper books, held their own magic. It was naked reading. There was nothing standing between her mind and the words.

Except the waiting, and the rising feeling of simultaneous panic and withdrawal. She had found lately that fear made her sleepy. She wondered whether anyone would notice if she just crawled under the waiting room seats, all attached to each other in a row, and went to sleep. She looked up at the counter. They would call her when they called her. There was nothing she could do. Her hands would shake with a real book. She had downloaded a free copy of the novel onto her phone awhile back. Now was the time to read it.

The Island of Doctor Moreau was a terrifying story. The protagonist, Edward Prendick, seemed sane, but the people on the island were not. Creepy things happened. There was suspense. Who knew what they were doing? Were they experimenting on animals? She was drawn in by the horror of it. For her whole life she had avoided stories of horrific happenings, the extremity of mankind's depravity, but now she sought it. She had started reading H. P. Lovecraft, sometimes in the middle of the night. When Chthulu was eating the planet, she could move her mind apart from herself. Other stories, the ones she thought she should be reading, didn't help anymore. And a tale about vivisection seemed eerily appropriate.

∽

April 1890

I must write Mother, thought Wells. Things were finally moving along for him. He grabbed a piece of stationery. "46 Fitzroy Road," he wrote at the top. A respectable address. She'd been proud that he was a schoolmaster at Henley House School, and had a salary of £60 a year. And she always loved hearing from him.

He still had hopes for a degree. Studying on his own, however, was difficult. He'd bargained with Milne not to be in residence at Henley House School, so that he could have time to study. The new house provided a little more space for this, sharing as he was with Isabel and Aunt Mary. Oh, how he wanted to marry Isabel. But there just wasn't enough money to set up their own house.

Wells had managed, however, to pass the Intermediate Science exam. He'd earned a Second in Zoology. The Licentiate of the College of Preceptors was achieved also, along with a prize for his work, so now he should have full respect as an educationalist. He had to admit his thesis on Froebel was brilliant. Then he'd had a meeting with Milne. He was worth more now, he argued, and needed time to study. He confidently requested a £10 a year increase and reduced hours. The science master was popular, and Milne wanted the best for him, so he had agreed. Isabel and Aunt Mary had been delighted. The three of them had celebrated with a holiday in Whitstable. Everything could now focus on the Bachelor's exams.

But he needed a second, more flexible job, and it had fallen into his lap. A "mysterious communication" had arrived in January, from a William Briggs of the University Correspondence College, Cambridge. Briggs had read of Wells' recent success as a scholar. He invited him to come to Cambridge, at the college's expense, for a proposition that might interest him.

Wells had walked from the station to Parker's Piece. All these impressive buildings, he thought. The old universities. Excluded from them, he critiqued them from the outside. They had narrow thinking, he felt, years of stultified intellectual tradition focused on the classics. Good science had been done there, certainly, but the undergraduate curriculum was still grounded in classical subjects. To even study science here, he knew, you had to pass exams in Greek. It was ridiculous. I must write an article about that, he thought. He took a crumpled notebook out of his pocket and jotted down, "Greek for sci."

The University Correspondence College was an impressive Gothic pile. William Briggs met him at reception, and they shook hands.

"Mr. Wells," Briggs said heartily. "So glad you could come! Let me show you around, then we'll have a nice chat."

He led the way through the building.

"There are no students here at the moment," Briggs apologized. "All have gone home from our holiday session. We offer full residential programs during the holidays and in the summer. They're very popular with school masters and would-be school masters."

"Like myself," said Wells.

"Like yourself," smiled Briggs. At the end of the building, they came upon a large room with dozens of wooden cubby boxes along the wall. "This is the center of our correspondence operation," said Briggs. Three women were sorting packages into the cubbies. "Ah, and here's Jerry," said Briggs as the postman came in from the side entrance.

"Morning, Mr. Briggs," said Jerry, as he pulled out a stack of thick parcels from his bag.

"Morning, Jerry," said Briggs. "So, Mr. Wells, here you see what we do. Jerry here brings the post, and it's full of students' papers. Our girls here sort them into a cubby for each tutor. These are for our tutors who live here in town. They come by and collect them. But you'd be working from London, so out they go again to you by post."

"And all of this," said Wells, "is to help students with the University of London exams?"

"Most of it," said Briggs. "We also offer some civil service examination courses."

"How can it be a course," said Wells, "if it's all done by post?"

"That's the brilliant part," said Briggs, "and why I have built all this. So many people can't access the education they need to become middle-class schoolmasters. They already have day jobs, or other vocations. They're studying on their own, since the University offers the exams to anyone. But they need help, guidance, and often a plan for two years or more. The college provides the schedule and materials, and our tutors instruct by marking papers and sending them back to the students. You could be one of those tutors. We need a very good man for biology." He gestured Wells toward the courtyard, and they walked outside.

"So I would mark their papers telling them what they need to review, how to better understand what they're studying?"

"Exactly," said Briggs.

"How do they know what to study?" Wells was remembering his own efforts, his own "schema" pasted on the wall. He had worked by himself, except for his time at the

Normal School. It had not always been easy to know what to cover, or how to cover it, to properly prepare. The Bachelors exam loomed in his future, like some creature from another planet. But he could certainly help those taking the Matriculation and Intermediate tests.

"Well, here's what I've done," said Briggs. "I've taken several copies of the examinations, from the last four or five years. My staff has studied them and developed curriculum around them. That's what we provide to the students, and they practice with their papers."

Wells thought for a moment. It sounded easy, logical, and very much like cramming. He didn't like cramming. He felt it meant you didn't really learn anything. But he also saw the problem. All those men and women, many with a talent for science, some with a talent for teaching. All trapped in low-paying positions because they didn't have higher qualifications. People like himself, bright and scientifically-minded, but too poor to pay for a tutor or too far away from good help. They should have a chance, he thought. Same as anyone. A chance with a lot more help than I had.

"When do I start?" said Wells.

～

Katherine had been in Durham during the Brexit vote. Having dinner the night before with students at the university, she heard stories of fear. One was from Germany. Would he have to leave? Could he finish his degree? Another said he had a girlfriend in France. How would he see her? Could she come visit? That afternoon, she'd seen a march for Brexit. It had been very small, no more than two dozen people. Some of them looked tough, with tattoos and vests and slouch hats. They carried a sign and were laughing and shouting loudly. Most people ignored them. Might not be a good idea, she thought.

The next morning, she talked to Sally at the hotel on Claypath. This was her new favorite place to stay. Even though she was on her own, they had given her a suite. The room was clean but old, with uneven floors and nowhere to write but the bed. The first night, the room had become uncomfortably warm. Katherine had been unable to get the heat to turn off, even though she turned the dial on the radiator all the way down. She had to come down to the desk in her pajamas to get someone to turn it off, and had woken Donald, who owned the hotel.

Donald was middle class and somewhat posh, his suit fitting his lean body perfectly. Sally, who worked at the hotel, was working class. Both were local. Down in the breakfast room, Sally would cook for everyone in the morning, then clean the rooms in the afternoon. She was an older woman, Katherine thought, and shouldn't work so hard. Katherine was saddled with the middle-class American difficulty in recognizing people's place. When she'd first returned to England, just out of high school, she'd visited a friend of her mother's. The kindly woman, gray-haired and well into her eighties, insisted on Katherine sitting in the front room, while she placed various dishes through a hole in the wall from the kitchen, then came around and served. Here with Sally, since Katherine woke late and was usually the last customer, she'd take her dishes to the kitchen and talk to Sally while she washed up, then tell her she'd left her room neat and there was no need to clean. Sally was surprised but grateful.

The morning of the vote, she asked both of them what they thought of Brexit. Donald said, "I'm voting Remain, of course," and went off to do business in town. Sally said, "I want Brexit. I really do. But I talked to my grandchildren. They said Remain would be better for them, to be part of Europe. I want to vote for the next generation, not for me."

After breakfast, Katherine walked through Market Square on the way to Waterstones, the one where they sell Durham University merchandise. There were Remain campaigners in the square, handing out stickers. They asked if she'd like one and she accepted, taking both a sticker and a larger flyer that said Remain. She put the sticker on her cardigan, and the flyer in her clear plastic folder, with the sign showing out the side. As she waited to cross at the corner, a bus came by and stopped at the light. A young man sitting near the rear of the bus looked down at her. He saw her folder, and her sign. He smiled and held up a cautionary finger, shaking it at her. No, he was saying, you've got it wrong. She smiled back and, aware of her tourist status, turned the folder around.

She decided to go back across the square and buy a newspaper at W. H. Smith. *The Times* confidently announced that Remain would win, that Brexit had no chance. They had charts and graphs, all very convincing.

That night she met the students at a tapas restaurant on Silver Street. She'd never had tapas and was worried because she was allergic to cured meat. But the staff was very kind and told her all the dishes that had it. She was seated in the middle of a long table, with university staff and students around her.

And all of them enjoyed that she was American. Yes, they had Brexit woes, they said. But you have that crazy billionaire who just got nominated. Trump, was it? Yes, she said. He couldn't actually be president, could he? He could, she said. He's tapped into the same sort of uneducated populace as your Brexit. No, they said. Not possible. He's an idiot. Yes, she said, like quite a few voters.

By the next morning, everyone knew Brexit had won, by a narrow margin. She could see the shock in people's faces near the university. But Durham is not just its university. Because of her heavy bag, Katherine needed a cab to take her to the train. Sally called a friend who had a cab, and he came to pick her up. As they bounced along the cobble stones and down the hill, she decided to ask him about Brexit. Carefully.

"Are you a happy voter or a sad voter today?" As was common, he asked her to repeat what she said, struggling with her accent. He said something she asked him to repeat, because the phrase was so unusual. "I'm over the moon!" he exclaimed. "Finally, we'll get away from Europe. They've been stealing us blind. Now we'll get the money back from them, and it'll go to the National Health. That's where it's needed. It will help everybody!"

"Good idea," she said. Because it was a good idea. It just didn't happen to be true.

And five months later America would enter an era of incivility that would make truth look negotiable.

8

The train went from Durham to Newcastle, of course, but Katherine decided she'd rather take the bus. Better view and better eavesdropping on a bus, and cheaper too. So she walked across Elvet Bridge, through the heart of town, across the Framwellgate Bridge, and down to the bus station, waiting at Bay 5.

Busses always surprised her. Sometimes she'd be expecting an old city bus, and a large coach would pull up, with steps up to the best seats. Other times a double-decker would park, shiny and new, with curved stairs winding up and a panoramic front window.

It was a hot day, and she paid the driver exact change (always appreciated) and went upstairs, thrilled to get the window at the front. The street was a sheer drop below her feet. The bus left Durham, heading out onto the road. She was dressed lightly, but as they headed north, the sun began beating in the window.

At the first stop, a couple climbed up and took the opposite seat, also in the front window.

The ride went on, through villages and rural areas, a few people on here or off there, with a pause and a break for the driver to smoke at Chester-le-Street. By this point, the front window had turned into an oven, and Katherine was sweating. But the passengers behind her were going on about what a nice day it was, so she tried to go with that, but it was just too hot. The couple up front with her had taken off their sandals, and had their feet against the glass, basking in the sunshine.

Katherine thought back to her first time in London, when she was eighteen. After a week of rain, the sun had come out in the city at lunchtime. She had watched astonished as staid British workers came out of the office buildings, stripping off shirts and hose as they headed toward the park. As she walked past the offices, every strip of grass displayed white British skin, roasting in the sun. People lying in the park, half-naked, to catch some rays, white brassieres glittering.

They're nuts, she thought, dripping sweat as the couple in the front window toasted their toes. Moving back to the next row, she caught a flash of brown out the window. A huge statue, arms spread wide. The Angel of the North, and so close. They must be off the main road.

Newcastle bus station, Eldon Square, was attached to a shopping mall, so the air conditioning was a relief. Crossing through, she walked toward the art gallery, which she'd seen from the bus. It was closed. She realized she didn't know where she was now, and the Google map wasn't helpful in the bright sunlight. She went into a W. H. Smith, to the back, looking for a mini-map of the city. There weren't any, and no one to ask, the non-electronic tills backed up with customers. By now she was in the city center, surrounded by beautiful white buildings. I'll try Waterstones. She came in and went up to the front counter.

The girl, young, with jet black hair and two piercings in her lip, looked up and smiled.

"You okay?" she said. This, Katherine had learned, was the universal greeting.

"Yes, thanks. Do you have a map please?"

"A map?"

"Yes please."

"Of where?"

"Here."

The girl looked puzzled, and pointing downward at her Doc Martens repeated, "Here?"

"Yes, please. Newcastle. Do you have one?"

"Oh! No one ever asks for a map of *here*. I dunno," she said, looking around on the counter. A stack of mini-maps came into view. "Oh! Here it is. No one ever asked before. Looks like we have them." As she left, Katherine overheard the girl say to a colleague, "She wanted a map of *here*."

Onward to the river.

As in Durham, Katherine presumed she would find the river a calming influence. And she knew about the bridges, from watching *Vera* on television. The walk took her downhill, through less prosperous parts of the old town. At one corner, she had to step into the street, because the pavement bricks were all broken. As she approached, a beggar was sitting on the ground with his cap out. The only people around were builders and laborers, all men. She wasn't comfortable giving money in this place, but as she walked past him the begging man said, "Careful, love — the pavement's torn up" and she felt badly for walking on.

It was a long way down the hill, and she wondered how she would get the energy to return back up. She walked along the embankment, enjoying the Vera bridges, and ended up waiting for a bus to take her back up the hill. A vaping man and an older woman were waiting.

"Why don't you stop smoking those things?" said the woman. "It's disgusting."

"They're healthy," he said.

"They're not healthy," she replied. "They're smoking. It's bad for you."

He began to get irritated.

"Look, they're not like regular cigarettes. It's more like water vapor."

"Call it what you like, it's smoking. It's not good for your lungs."

"Mum, I told you. It's healthier. It's not burning, see?"

"If your father were alive, he'd tell you it's smoking. He'd know, wouldn't he?"

"Mum, come on. You need to read about things. Everyone knows these are much better for you. Not like smoking at all."

"You're wrong." Both their voices were rising as they argued.

"I'm not, you silly cow." Katherine winced, but mum came right back.

"You're an ungrateful boy, and you shouldn't be smoking so much."

The bus arrived. They argued all the way up the hill to the station.

Making her way through the blessedly cool shopping mall, Katherine waited just a few minutes for the bus. The sun was going down now, so she raced back upstairs for the front window. The next few stops, teenagers got on, just out of school. They climbed up and looked a bit perplexed when they saw her; this must have been their usual section of the bus. They sat in the other seats, a bit away.

At Chester-le-Street, the bus pulled up beside a young man carrying a plastic tote bag. He got on, and they all heard the driver say, as the door closed, "That's a hot meal, is it?"

"Yeah," said the man, "lucky to get it too. They close in five minutes."

"Well you can't eat it on here."

"I what?"

"You can't eat it on here. The smell. It's awful."

They heard the man grunt, and he came upstairs.

"Hi, girls," he said to the teenagers, only two of whom were girls. Then, as he headed back to his seat, he said, "Who does he think he is? Can't eat my tea, eh? I just got off work. Been working all day." There was a rustle of the plastic bag, and the smell of curry suffused the air. He continued, as he arranged his food. "He thinks he's the government, eh? He's just a bus driver. Telling me I can't eat my tea. Is that right, I ask you? I ask you?" he said to the girls. They said, "no" quietly, and went back to their conversation.

Katherine assumed he would stop nattering to eat his meal, but he continued. His language got worse, till the teenagers were at first giggling and then just trying not to be shocked. He also got louder, and the smell stronger. The bus back to

Durham wasn't as pleasant as the trip out had been, even with seeing The Angel of the North up close.

❧

Newcastle? said Wells. What about that accent?

Oh, I rarely have trouble with accents, said Katherine. Unless they're very thick.

I had trouble with mine, said Wells. A cockney accent, lower-class Bromley. And with my higher register, it was particularly bothersome. I worked hard to do away with it, sound more like Londoners. I managed it in the end.

Yes, said Katherine, people do remark on your voice. It seems to get higher when you get agitated about something.

Yes. . . the only time it was considered too posh was when I was in Wales. There my English accent made me a marked man. Probably why that boy fouled me so badly at Holt.

You thought yourself superior?

They thought that I did, he said. Well, maybe I did. Maybe I was.

Indeed, said Katherine.

He smiled.

❧

Since the Liang Art Gallery had been closed on her first visit to Newcastle, Katherine was determined to see it on the next trip. She happily took the bus again from Durham, alighting right outside the gallery. It was not Sunday, so the gallery was open. The entrance was confusing, if it was in fact the entrance. Glass doors led into a ramp and down into the gift shop. The gallery was behind.

But she was hungry and headed for the café directly. She noticed only the food, ordering soup and cake and tea. Finding a table, she studied the gallery map. Gradually she saw that some people were coming into the café, but not eating. They were looking at a stained-glass window mounted in the corner. Cake first, she thought.

An older couple moved carefully toward their table from the till. The man, tall and with white hair, cautiously balanced the tray. It had two pots of tea, two small milk jugs, a sugar cube bowl with tongs, and two boxed sandwiches. His progress was perilous. Katherine realized that jumping up to help would be ridiculous. The wife bowled ahead to find a table and began removing things from herself. Head scarf, purse, coat. Everything easily filled a table for four, even though they were only two.

It felt odd for Katherine to take her tray to the rack, put her dishes there, and then walk through all the tables to get to the stained-glass object. It was a lovely window with what looked like angels. "Sir Edward Coley Burne-Jones, 1896," said the sign. Oh! Pre-Raphaelite. So everything looks like angels anyway. The first pane had a figure with "Caritas" written above it, the next pane "Fortitudo" with a figure holding a shield shot full of arrows. Below Caritas was a man kneeling on the floor in misery with two figures looking on, and below Fortitudo was a king. Then divided between the panes at the bottom was a dedication. On the left, it was to a man named Gibson who had died at age 39 in November 1894. On the right, to his children: Phoebe who had died in February 1892 and Rex who had died in July 1894. Katherine's heart gave a twist. His children had pre-deceased him.

The incredibly sad, very beautiful window was in the café. People drank their tea and ate their boxed sandwiches. Next to them as they studied their gallery maps was a memorial to a man who had lost his children. She wondered which mourning family member had been left to commission it.

She walked from the cafe in the direction of a special gallery called Northern Spirit. There were beautiful paintings by artists she had never heard of. Louis H. Grimshaw, John Martin, Thomas Bewick, John Wilson Carmichael. As she noted paintings she liked especially, she realized they were all by the same painter, Ralph Hedley. *Last in the Market*, of a cherubic boy asleep next to his dog, holding a basket. An old couple saying grace by a window, looking for all the world like a Northeast England version of a Vermeer. A man standing in his front room, holding a baby. All of them images of ordinary people in a local setting, all of the works showing a deep understanding of human nature. His *Blinking in the Sun (Cat in the Cottage Window)* she later saw on a t-shirt. How could she never have heard of him?

A north that the south neglects, a north that some see as crime-ridden, the home of both Brexiteers and multicultural neighborhoods, held treasures beyond castles, cathedrals, and scenery. Culture, Wells had said, is preserved by the wealthy. Whoever had preserved these, she was grateful.

∽

July 1890

It was time to take the tram home, and Wells was very tired. He had finally recovered from his cold. He had been miserable, trying to balance marking papers, teaching laboratories, and studying for exams, all with a scratchy throat and a head stuffed with wool. He had thought then, not for the first time, that he could die. Many died from pneumonia, of course. Colds could start innocently enough, and end in the mortuary. There was just no telling with germs. Perhaps he could write a story about it. A scientist could have a toxic bacillus in a lab, something that could kill everyone in the world. And it could be stolen. Instead, Wells had written such a despairing letter to Simmons that he quite frightened him and had to send another assuring Tommy of his good attitude.

The horse tram went from the corner of Strand and Aldwych, a short distance from the laboratory classroom at Booksellers Row, to Camden High Street, a moderate walk from the flat. At a penny a mile for three miles, it was better than walking. Wells had just finished teaching the evening biology class. It was a warm evening, and by the time he got to the corner he was perspiring. Stepping up into the tram car, he took a seat downstairs near the door. The tram was crowded with people leaving work. As it filled, the car became unpleasantly hot. And yet, as they rode up Kingway, he became aware that people who got on did not sit near him. Indeed, after a mile or so he noticed that most were sitting bunched together near the other end of the tram.

Is it me? thought Wells. Perhaps I look ill and sweaty. They think I have a tropical fever. He touched his brow. It felt warm, of course, given the weather. But not clammy. Three people disembarked at Holborn. Four got on, and a young lady with a blue hat stopped as if to sit next to him, then moved on. That's it, he thought. They think I'm the Whitechapel murderer. But it's been two years since he killed last, surely. Truly, they are shrinking from my presence. Do they think I'm the devil, in a clever disguise?

He got out his handkerchief, to wipe his brow a bit so he could look more comfortable. He noticed his hand smelled like fish. It dawned on him that all of him smelt like fish. They'd been dissecting dogfish all evening. Good heavens, he must smell horrific. Well, that's the life of a biological demonstrator, he thought. If we want scientific progress in this country, they'll just have to get used to it. Besides, there's more room for my feet.

༄

Katherine had begun looking for Wells' writings from the *Henley House School Magazine*, and after much online searching, realized that there were only two places that had them: the University of Illinois (which had purchased Wells' papers), and Yale University. Neither, upon inquiry, would make any copies for her.

But the British Studies conference that year was in Providence, so it wouldn't be too difficult to rent a car and go to Yale. The day was glorious, sunny and beautiful for autumn, although there was little of that colorful foliage she'd always read about. The drive was easy, on highways and through wonderful little towns.

She had rented the car at a place underneath the conference hotel in Providence. The small office in the garage was plain and gloomy, and she had to wait behind a couple renting a convertible. The young man helping them (university age, perhaps?) was patient. They were quite chatty, and they had to think long and hard about the contract to rent. Did they want insurance? He didn't know but thought perhaps that was covered by her credit card. She wanted to be sure they would be covered, so they asked a great many questions. Then, once the key was handed over, the young man asked where they were planning to go, and a long discussion ensued about all the things they were going to do with the car. Katherine felt quite invisible, and looked around for another assistant, but no one seemed to be there but the one man.

Upon getting to the front of the queue, Katherine filled out forms as quickly as possible, and didn't engage in chat. This was to prove a mistake. The attendant walked her out to the car. She was not accustomed to new cars, since she didn't consider them as status symbols but rather efficient (or not) modes of transport. The ignition was keyless, the young man explained. You hold the fob here and it starts. No problem, she said. Do I return it to this spot? Yes, the man said. Fine. Goodbye.

She did not stop anywhere on the way to Yale University Library, wanting to get there quickly. One never knows with archives. Things might be efficient, or they might take all day. She found a spot to park in a shopping area near the school and walked over to the ridiculously modern building that held all the old books. There were lockers for her things, the security guard said. Please bring only pencils and paper into the archive. She locked up her things and went upstairs.

What is it with glass doors in archives? I suppose they want to see everyone and everything going on, she thought. Another security guard searched her things, opening her notebook between every page. It felt invasive. Odd, she thought, that this should feel more exposed than when she was patted down at the airport for refusing to go through the body scanner. Finally, she was approved and given her books, already waiting, and pointed toward another set of glass doors.

It didn't take long to find the articles, and she spent an hour or so discovering interesting things. Henley House School, she knew, had been run by J. V. Milne. He had been father to A. A. Milne who, she found, was only one of several sons. They all attended the school, of course. Their marks were published each year, and Katherine couldn't help but notice that A. A.'s marks were not as high as those of his older brothers. That must have been tough, she thought. No wonder he wrote such things about his dad in his autobiography.

She read a column about a school visit to the zoo. It didn't mention H. G. specifically, but it said the teacher took them, and the description of the outing sounded like something Wells would lead as the only science teacher. It occurred to her that Wells may have been the reason for A. A. seeing his first bear, but she couldn't prove it.

Having taken a number of photographs of pages, she closed everything carefully, returned the books to the desk, said thank you, went to the lockers, then left. Hungry, she noticed a crepe place right in the parking lot, and went in. A young and lovely woman, with an accent (African? Caribbean?) took her order. The entire place was run only by her. After the only other customer left with his crepe, Katherine sat down at the counter to order hers. Where are you from, she asked.

"Brazil," said the girl. She expertly made the crepes.

"This place is very French," said Katherine, noting the Parisian decor. "Have you been to France?"

"Once," she said, "but only for a short time. My mother was French."

"Are you at the university?"

"Yes. I'm studying science and philosophy." She launched into a long explanation of the things she enjoyed learning, and how excellent the Yale professors were. Her voice was lovely, and the words flowed in a steady, pleasant stream.

"What would you like to do after you get your degree?" Katherine asked, as she took another bite of cheese and crepe.

"Well." The girl suddenly looked shy. "I'm not sure. You see, I wanted to be a teacher, but…" she looked like she might start to cry.

Katherine went through in her mind all the reasons one couldn't be a teacher. None of them seemed to apply here. "Why not?"

"I was born with a speech problem. My parents put me in therapy in Brazil for a long time. So really, I can't be a teacher, because of that."

Katherine was completely perplexed. The girl was quite serious. And she spoke beautifully.

She said, gently, "What level would you want to teach? Small children? Teens?"

There were tears, just glinting on her lower lid, not falling, and she was still smiling politely and her voice was level but quiet. "What I'd really like is to be a professor, like the ones I have in my classes here."

Katherine paused, then spoke slowly, choosing words carefully. You have been handed someone's dream, she thought. Don't crush it by laughing, or you'll be misunderstood.

"I am a professor," said Katherine. "Not at a big university like this. At a small college. And I can assure you, I would not have known about the speech problem if you hadn't told me. I do not hear a problem now. I cannot see why you couldn't be a professor if you worked hard and wanted to."

The girl looked stunned. And then she really did start to cry. Katherine was very glad there was no one else in the shop.

"Really?" she sniffed. "Are you serious?"

"Yes, I'm quite sure. And more than your talking, you are bright and articulate and interested in so many things. I'm quite sure you could do this, and you must stop thinking that you can't."

"But my mother said…"

"I think your mother would be quite proud if you did it."

Katherine gave her a business card, and said, "I'd love to hear from you as you go through school. I have every confidence in you." She paid, and left the girl in tears, and saying thank you so much, I can't thank you enough.

Katherine got to the car and waved the fob at the door. She got in, then realized she didn't know how to start the vehicle. Where a key should be, for the ignition, there was nothing at all. She waved the fob uselessly in front of the steering wheel. She leaned over to check in the glove box for instructions, but there was nothing but the placard from the rental car place. She tried to look up the car make and model on her phone, but couldn't find anything, so she called the rental car place, and someone actually picked up. Yes, it is the fob, they said. You hold it up on the panel under the dash. Thank you, she said.

But she couldn't find the fob now. How was that possible? She looked outside the car door. Had she dropped it when she got in? Slipped it in the glove box looking for the instruction book? Lost it under the seat? She walked around the car, kneeled by the open doors. She got in to the driver's seat again and leaned her head against the wheel. Well, that's no use, she thought.

The crepe had been salty. She picked up her water bottle and there it was, underneath. Flat and disk-like, black like the surface at the bottom of the cup-holder, it had simply disappeared. Well, she thought, as she reversed the car and got back on the road, I got some work done and I helped someone. Then I lost my tiny mind. Fine.

When she got back to California and printed the photos from the archive, she discovered that she had missed the last line of the piece she wanted to reprint in her book. It would take a pleading email to the archivist, and $5 on her credit card, before the work would be completed.

∽

January 1891

Wells knew it couldn't possibly be the dullness of his life that brought it on, but the hemorrhage seemed connected somehow. More likely it was the intense work he'd done for the Bachelor's degree examinations. He knew that studying wasn't easy, of course. The trouble was, he spent most of his time helping others do it. The correspondence college papers came in continually. He marked them in the park, at the flat in Fitzroy Road, at the coffee house. He tried to write encouraging notes. But he was depressed by the low level of ability demonstrated in many of the papers. Sometimes he despaired of a scientific worldview ever emerging from a nation with such dull minds. The combination of studying and marking papers began to remove him from real life. He barely spoke to Isabel or his aunt. His letters to Simmons and Elizabeth Healey slowed to a trickle.

How he missed them, his old classmates. He would go out occasionally, to an exhibit opening or science lecture, and was disappointed when they weren't there. He wished he hadn't been so stupid. How could he give away his life at the Normal School of Science, now the Royal College of Science? And yet Tommy Simmons had done the same, in a sense. He had been a science lecturer for three years but was preparing to take his Bachelor's exams at the same time as Wells. The difference was that Simmons had been earning decent money, while Wells was still struggling to write. His last letter to Simmons before he took the exams had been despairing. No one seemed to want his work. He'd done the odd educational review, but nothing had been requested from the *Educational Times* or *Saturday Review*. Winter was closing in when he finally took the examinations.

The lung hemorrhage in December just seemed to confirm how far Wells was from his goals. He had his coveted Bachelor of Science at last and could put both B.Sc. and L.C.P. by his name on articles, if there were any. He didn't have enough money to marry Isabel, or even think about starting his own household. But Dr. Collins had come through again, securing him several weeks recovery at Uppark. Here he relaxed, knowing he was in good hands. Once again, he began to read.

9

What am I doing all this for? thought Katherine, as she tried to put aside a lecture she was writing, to get back to the Wells book. She had made another cup of tea and was sitting in her favorite chair. Sunlight gleamed through the front window, so much so that she had to close the drape half-way to see the screen. I shouldn't be writing this now, she thought. There is so much else to do.

In fact, even with a cup of tea, this is all quite discouraging. I've been working on Wells for almost three years. I have applied for three major grants and a minor one and been turned down for all. Only a few friends and colleagues even know I do this. And whenever anyone hears about Wells, they assume I'm writing about science fiction.

Well you should, he said. My scientific romances were quite good.

But I'm discouraged, she said. I want to be a serious writer, a non-fiction writer. I wish I'd gone to Columbia. I wish I had become Lionel Shriver.

Then I shall tell you about the *Fortnightly Review*, he said. It was 1891. I was so happy that they had published my "Rediscovery of the Unique" in July, that I sent Frank Harris another essay. I wanted to be a serious writer, a science writer, what you call non-fiction. But when he received my second article, he summoned me to his office. And do you know what happened?

I recall something about a hat, she said.

Yes, I didn't have any proper clothes for a meeting with an important editor. I hadn't met anyone important really, you know. My writings had been for school magazines where I knew everyone, or letters for the *Educational Times*. Frank Harris was something else entirely. I wanted to look appropriate, and I had very little money, and no idea of style. I felt I should at least have a silk hat and an umbrella, but both were pretty shabby. My aunt and I tried to make the hat look good, and ultimately I had patted it down with a wet cloth against her advice.

I was very nervous, and Harris began to grill me about my article, which he didn't understand at all, but I had put my hat down on the table between us and we were both distracted by it. As it dried, the hat got fuzzier and fuzzier. I tried to ignore it but I was too nervous. I didn't answer his questions properly, and he refused the article and sent me away. I didn't write anything serious for a year.

Yes, said Katherine. And when you did you began writing fiction, and you enjoyed it.

My point is, said Wells, that discouragement is not permanent. Perhaps it is necessary.

᠊ᢅ᠊

Through the glass doors at the oh-so-modern Cambridge library. You could feel the air conditioning. Special Collections.

"Good morning," Katherine said to the man behind the desk. He was seated, and older, with an expression of deep patience but little wrinkles that suggested a sense of humor. Perhaps he left it at home for safe-keeping.

"Good morning," he said. "How may I be of assistance?"

"I ordered Box 776 for today," she said. "Nineteenth-century educational papers."

"Ah yes," he said. "I'm afraid it isn't just one box. You'll also need box 779. I have both here, but you can only take them out one at a time. Which would you like first?"

"Box 776 please. I didn't know there would be more, but that's good."

"Your reader's card please?"

Katherine proudly took it from her bag. It had been obtained that morning.

Reader's cards, she had found, had become important to her perception of herself as a researcher. They meant she was more than just a college teacher. In England on holiday, she had seen tourists swarming around the libraries in Oxford and Cambridge as the real scholars edged their way through the door to treasures unseen. She wanted to be one of those scholars and had investigated how to get the cards.

At the British Library, she had to join a long queue, and create an application on the computer, then be interviewed about what she intended to research. But the card was free, and had her picture, and didn't expire for a long time. At Cambridge it was more complicated, but nothing special. She had to show a letter from her college, saying that she was permanently employed there. Oxford demanded the same letter, plus a high fee and the somewhat theatrical oath.

"Here you are," the archivist said. "Box 776."

She took the box back to a table and laid it down carefully. At first, it was not clear how to open the box. It slid out of a sleeve, then had to be turned over and placed just so to wiggle out a half box inside. It was filled with papers of various sizes, colors, and thicknesses, separated by beige-colored cardstock. Advertisements for schools, letters about school reports. This was Cambridge, so she was hoping for something about the University Correspondence College, maybe even a prospectus or letter. The catalog had said this box was specifically for extended education. But it was a disorganized collection of items. A typed paper on pedagogy, a booklet from a secretarial school, a newspaper article on a training school that had closed.

Carefully folding it all back up again, she took it up to the desk.

"Will you be needing this again?" the archivist asked.

"No, thank you. I'm only here for the one day."

"Are you sure?" he said, looking at her intently.

Katherine hesitated. She didn't want to offend him. If it was usual for people to have a box held for them, she wanted to do what was usual. But she knew she wouldn't need anything that was in the box. She'd just been through it, one item at a time.

"I ask," he said, "because we do send these back directly to the vaults. Often times people tell us they don't need them, and then they find out they do after all."

"Thank you, but I really don't think —"

"I will save this for you for the rest of the day, just in case," he decided. "Would you like the other box now?"

"Yes, please."

Knowing better now how to manage boxes, she returned to the same table. Much the same sort of thing, really. She carefully turned everything over, one item at a time, taking a few notes. Carefully putting everything back one page at a time, she closed the box, and began to gather her things. I'll just give this back, and go find the tea room, she thought. But she couldn't find her reader's card.

She checked her bag. She opened her computer in case it had gotten folded into the laptop. She surreptitiously checked on her seat, under the table. In the box with the slips of paper. It wasn't anywhere.

Trying not to panic, she thought, I know — it must have slipped between the pages when I returned them to the box. I'll go through everything again.

The next twenty minutes were spend carefully turning each page from the box. Nothing.

Oh, no, she thought, it's gotten into the first box!

She returned to the desk.

"You were right," she said, with a smile. "I do need the other box back." She was far too embarrassed to say why, especially when he nodded sagely in an I-told-you-so kind of way. He took the second box from her and returned with the first.

She took it back to the same table. Half an hour paging through again, one item at a time, looking for her card. Nothing. She sat there and stared at the box, knowing it was foolish to cry, or worry about paying for another card. She overheard another scholar at the desk, talking to the archivist.

"Hullo. I'm here to collect Box 92."

"Of course, sir. May I have your reader's card?"

He handed it to the archivist. Katherine watched as he went in the back and retrieved a box.

"Here you are, sir."

"May I have my card back, please?"

"I'm sorry, sir, but we keep the card for as long as you have the box."

Katherine exhaled. She got up from the table and handed the archivist the box. She told him she was finished for the day, and he handed her the card.

∽

December 1892

William Briggs puffed himself up.

"What do you think, Wells?" he asked. "Splendid, isn't it?"

Wells looked around the lab and could only approve. A big space, with lots of light, in the heart of London. All the laboratory equipment he could ask for: microscopes, balances, slide kits. "Excellent," he said.

"I'm so happy they had this property available," said Briggs. "All these little schools, secretarial, civil service, around the square. Just the sort of place we want. Less prestigious, mind you, than Cambridge. But printing 'Red Lion Square' on the prospectus says more than 'Booksellers Row'. Once the publishing operation is going fully at Foxton, we'll be producing all the text-books we need ourselves. By the way, how is it going on yours?"

"Just fine," said Wells. "I'm thinking of adding a whole section on evolution."

"At the end, surely?" said Briggs, eyebrows raised. "Wouldn't want that sort of thing up front."

They stood together admiring the view across the Square. They shared a birthday, so Briggs was exactly five years older than Wells. The Yorkshireman looked large and vigorous, a successful man of business. Wells, the scholar, was settling in. His collar was still a little big for his neck.

It was because of Briggs that Wells had earned enough money to marry Isabel, and he had done so the previous October. He planned to open his first real bank account after the holidays. Wells and Isabel loved each other, but temperamentally he knew there were problems. Sex hadn't been at all what he'd expected. It was a difficult business, a microcosm of their larger incompatibility. Her gentle, yielding nature didn't match his impulsiveness and passion.

The couple also disagreed about his work. Wells worried about the marking for the Correspondence College, worried about the kind of educational institution in which he was earning his pay. There were ethical issues he wanted to discuss with her. He had experienced the brilliant instructive lectures of T. H. Huxley personally, and had written numerous articles on the inadequacies of the science teaching of his age. Briggs's collegial operation surely had something of the charlatan to it, something akin to simply cramming with some outside help. It some ways it wasn't any different than Pitman's shorthand courses by post. At the same time, Wells so wanted to help young people who, like himself, were studying on their own to pass the exams and have a better life.

When he told Isabel that Briggs was running a cram college, fooling people and taking their money, she protested that he shouldn't say unkind things about his employer.

∽

Katherine checked the website before class to see if her medical test results were posted. She'd already checked a dozen times, and it was only noon.

How does one navigate the landscape between the test and the result? Why is that theme not everywhere? It's as if the mind erases that time, whether it's half an hour or two weeks. Even with scholarly exams. You remember the nervousness before the test, the frantic studying, and the result. But only rarely the space between. Oh yes, I was so scared, people say. Perhaps they were. But it isn't remembered viscerally, later.

It is a land I'm returning to, she thought, and I don't recall how I survived it before. Once she was in a second-hand book shop, one of many that was going out of business. One of the books was called "How to Survive Between Doctor Appointments." She'd always wished she'd bought it, but she hadn't.

The landscape is frightening, but it tries so hard to look normal. Just like an everyday place. And you have to walk through it because that's what time is, walking through things. How does one ignore the ghoulish figures that jump out of the damp grass? The specters of operating room staff swathed in winding sheets, the experts shaking their skeletal heads, popping up in front of your path. The sky is gray, with foreboding clouds. And yet you must walk it alone.

Perhaps if one could just concentrate, she thought. Instead of all these people, asking questions, expecting you to work normally. Today's another boring lecture, they think. She walks to class through a sticky, black pool. Her ankles can barely move in the muck. I should enjoy this, she thinks. I might not be doing it much longer. She raises her head at the podium to the dead eyes waiting for her to begin, smiles her morning smile and reaches for the roll sheet. But her lips pull back from her teeth as they often do when she sleeps, and her skin parches and starts to fall off, and the nails grow in unnatural shapes. They just see their usual prof, starting usual class, and they think about their friend and whether the prof would notice if they just sent one little text message.

Someone had said she should see a counselor. They're not trained in this space, she explained. They think of grief and loss as losing someone else. They don't know how the tin woodsman feels, losing body parts, disappearing before their eyes. To them, this waiting is just waiting, like waiting for a bus. But it's the formulation of nightmares that are waiting to become reality. A dim hope of reprieve that recedes the longer one waits. It's like waiting for someone to return from a war, except that the someone is you. Do you really think a clinical psychologist understands?

As a scholar, of course, she knew that millions would have gone through this, over the centuries. Help, if there was any, would be in their words, or the words of those who frame human misery. There were reflections on the Talmud, the deep knowledge of herbalists, the Spiritual Exercises of the Jesuits. There was Thomas Moore's *Dark Nights of the Soul* and Carolyn Myss's Jungian archetypes. She needed wisdom. But in this landscape of fear, she couldn't find the books.

✌

Heathrow Terminal 5 is so large that it is divided into three gate sections, with a train that takes people between them. The crowding on the platforms can be considerable. Once Katherine walked instead, when she saw an arrow pointing down a passage. It was incredibly long and she was exhausted when she arrived.

This time she took the train, walked through the UK/EU passport station, and was at baggage claim just before the bags came down. Having had some recent back problems, she looked around for help, and no one in any sort of uniform was around. So she sought out a hearty-looking young man to help her. One agreed, and when she saw her bag, he pulled it off the belt for her.

Grabbing the handle to pull it outward, she almost fell when the bag lurched. There was, she discovered, no fourth wheel. Bad back, three wheels, right after an eleven-hour flight which had followed a two-hour drive to LAX. Tipping the bag on the narrow edge, she struggled over to the nearest desk with helpful people looking at computers. Alas, they were not as helpful as all that.

"I'm sorry, but we are Iberia. You will need to go to the British Airways desk."

"Where is that?"

The man with the Iberia tag pointed far down the baggage claim area.

"How on earth will I get it there?" she asked. "I have a bad back."

He shrugged. She looked at the phone on his desk.

"Could you call someone to help me, please?" He shook his head and returned to his computer.

Grumbling that she'd never fly Iberia, Katherine tipped the bag again, but after several minutes was not making good progress. She saw a luggage cart and lifted the case onto it with some difficulty. Then she tried to push it. It was very hard to push, like it had a stuck wheel. Forcing it down the enormous room, she stopped at the first desk with "BA" on a sign.

"I need help," she said. "The baggage handlers broke the wheel on my bag."

"Yes, ma'am. You need to go to the baggage damage desk. They can repair your bag."

"And where is that?"

The woman with the BA tag pointed further down the room.

"But I can't push this cart anymore," she said. "Can someone get me another?" The woman looked around for someone, but at that moment Katherine noticed some words on the bar of the cart: "push down to move." She pushed down on the bar, and the wheels moved with ease.   She proceeded down to the far end of the room.

There was someone ahead of her, talking to a woman at the desk. There were two other assistants, but they were busy on computers. When it was her turn, she reported the problem, and was handed a form.

"Fill this in, please."

She filled in the form with her name, home address, mobile phone number, time of day, model of the bag, problem, flight number, flight time, passport number, and various other information.

"I've heard you might be able to repair my bag?"

The woman frowned at her form.

"This isn't a Samsonite?" It wasn't.

"I'm sorry, but we only repair the top models. We can offer you a replacement?"

"That would be fine, but I'd need the same size case. Do you have one?"

A case was wheeled out. It was much larger.

"I don't think I can manage this. It's very large."

Another case was wheeled out. It was smaller than the one she had. She began to feel like Goldilocks in an unfriendly ursine house.

"I can't do that one. My things won't fit."

"I'm sorry, ma'am. You'll have to take the larger one."

"I can't manage the larger one. Is there any way mine can be repaired elsewhere?"

The woman handed her another form.

"If you fill this out, you will be contacted tomorrow at home. They can come to your house and repair it."

"Home? I'll be at a flat, but it isn't mine. I'm visiting."

The woman looked confused. "If you live outside London, we can bring it to your house. Just put down your home address."

I'm jet-lagged, Katherine thought. Is baggage repair only for those who live here? They never break the bags of visitors?

Fine, she thought, I'll struggle this beast onto the Underground, and get it to the flat. She gave the attendant her phone number.

"They'll call you tomorrow."

Katherine knew perfectly well she'd be at the British Library tomorrow. She began her walk to the tube, the bag lurching dangerously as she went around corners.

She was in Saltaire, a place she'd never been before. Her research said it would be a good, safe location, close enough to transport through the Yorkshire Dales. It was a place of historical interest, where entrepreneur Titus Salt had built a town for his mill workers. She had not realized at the time how much of an enclave it was, situated among post-industrial towns and the city of Bradford. The flat she had rented was dirty. The vacuum cleaner, once found in an upstairs closet, was filthy. It had been raining a lot and the carpet smelled of mold.

She looked out the kitchen window, into the courtyard. A few yards away were sheds she now knew had once been privies for multiple families. The sun had come out, and someone looked back at her. A white cat sat on the privy wall, looking in her window. He had a supremely confident air. This was clearly his yard, and his house to watch, and his responsibility to keep an eye on her. It was not a friendly glare, but she liked cats so much it didn't matter. She felt somehow protected.

I like cats too, said Wells, beside her at the sink. Never could understand the passion for dogs. Dogs are no help at all when you're trying to write. They always want to be taken outside.

Cats aren't much help either, she replied. My cat at home is continually blocking my screen and vying for my attention.

Mine is named Mr. Peter Wells, he said. He's wonderful with guests. If they talk for too long or become annoying, he meows, puts his nose in the air, and leaves the room as if they've offended him. But dogs, dogs are confused. They are too much like people. No mind of their own.

Perhaps, she said looking across the yard into the green feline eyes, I am being found wanting.

Yes, he said. To cats, we are usually insufficient.

10

No pension, no cottage, no thank you, nothing. Sarah was again at the train station in Petersfield. Her feet hurt, as they had unaccountably for months. Her joints ached, and now at age seventy-one she was sure it was rheumatism. And people spoke so poorly nowadays, so low and indistinct. She couldn't always hear them when they asked her to do something. What would she do now? Joe was in his happy, idle laziness at Nyewoods, living in the cottage she had been paying for. The boys were all right, but she'd had to help them out several times, even sending meat at Christmas.

Twelve years, and no thank you. That woman thought that Sarah had been saying things about the family. Well, maybe she had. She couldn't remember. She couldn't remember a lot of things anymore. But she remembered that her "mistress" was just a dairy maid's sister who had moved up in the world through marriage. Sarah might have held that against her, perhaps after another refusal of a ride to church. She'd been so loyal, and now it was just her and her suitcase again, at the station. God, she hoped, would find a way.

She'd return to Bertie's house in London. Back to the Haldon Road house where she'd been just a month before, taking a little holiday. Her boy was finally married, and to such a nice respectable woman, a cousin. Joe's brother had been a

112

nice man, and his daughter was lovely and polite. Perhaps there would be grandchildren, she thought as the train took her into the city.

Bertie and Isabel were pleased to see her, if dismayed at the reason. Sarah had grown stout on the cakes and scones in the kitchen, but as always she looked pale. She walked with great effort. Those underground passages where she'd worked, thought H. G., had not been good to her. Between the lack of sunlight and the damp, she'd grown even older than her years. He was proud he could provide shelter for her. But he had no idea what to do about her, or his brothers. He'd just got word that Freddy's job was more precarious than it had appeared, and Frank had moved in with their father at Nyewoods. Frank made a pittance repairing watches.

It's all right, he thought. We'll get Mother back with Father at Nyewoods, and I'll find a way to help pay their rent. We'll go visit in the spring.

But the fact was he was distracted. Just a few months ago, he had begun his afternoon biology laboratory class at the Tutorial College. It had been more difficult than he had anticipated. He helped equip the laboratories, but it was hard to find good microscopes for less than five guineas. He also had to carry his correspondence students' booklets back and forth to class, marking them when he could. He'd gotten efficient, writing comments at a rate of about twenty minutes per booklet. He was pleased to be doing what he saw as undermining unreasonable and fact-focused examiners.

But marking wasn't the distraction. In his class, two young women were sharing a table. If either had been alone, he knew, he would not have spoken to them much. But together they seemed more approachable. And Miss Robbins, the smaller of the two, was so appealing. She was bright, and interested in learning, and was preparing to take her own examinations. Her ambition and humor and intelligence were such a contrast to serious Isabel, who never seemed to dream. He had such dreams.

Amy Catherine is making me ambitious again, he thought. Why should I settle for this life? She has recalled me to myself, as a man with a future. I would like that future to be with her.

❧

"It must be difficult," said the counselor, crossing his legs, "to always be the smartest person in the room."

He looked oddly nondescript sitting there. Katherine had not been sure what to expect, but certainly not someone who appeared so outwardly professional and so inwardly damaged. That's the story with psychologists, she thought. They're all crazy.

"I'm not at all the smartest person in the room," she said, "just often out of place."

"But you are concerned with your mental capacity?"

"Yes," she said. "With the medication, I had a lot of trouble thinking straight. Even staying awake. I was hoping you could help me get my balance back, and some perspective."

"I can," he said, and for several weeks he plied her with photocopied handouts. It seemed like each appointment, she spent much time explaining. She needed help reestablishing cognitive ability, analyzing herself and the world more objectively. It was a process of re-entry, like a spaceship.

The counselor, however, had recently rejected such a rational approach in his own life. He'd been through trauma of his own. So instead he encouraged her to overcome the focus on cognition. The key to happiness was inner peace. And the key to inner peace was developing a larger view.

"Don't worry," he said. "This isn't about religion. Or even spirituality. But it is ultimately about rejecting the cognitive, and developing the broader aspects of the self."

She tried, using the worksheets. Her goal was different, however, and she quickly became frustrated. Perhaps she was supposed to have an interest in the expansion of the mind and heart. Perhaps she would at a later time. But when you're just trying to think straight, it was maddening.

She tried different analogies. I've lost my moorings, she explained. I don't need a new ocean, just the ability to berth the boat I have already. I'm trying to reclaim myself, she said, the self I was. I don't want to create a new self. I liked my old self. Ultimately, she said, the goal is to be able to once again think on my feet. I want to get through a lecture without losing my train of thought. A new track isn't needed, just some fresh coal for the old locomotive.

He gave her a handout about karma and self-awareness.

∾

May 1893

Wells was carrying fossils, and they weighted him down like rocks. He had just been helping a young man studying geology. It had been a long day. Walking up Villiers Street to catch his train at Charing Cross, he began coughing. He tasted blood.

This hadn't happened in many months. No, it can't be, he thought. He put a handkerchief to his mouth and got on the train. The compartment was empty. His handkerchief was turning scarlet. He got off at Putney Bridge to walk home. The coughing stopped. I refuse to believe it's another hemorrhage, he thought. I'm hungry and I want a big dinner first in case anyone makes a fuss. He came home, hid his handkerchief in his coat pocket, kissed Isabel and Aunt Mary, and enjoyed a hearty meal of chops, potatoes and spinach. But in the night the cough began again. This is impossible, he thought. I have to lecture tomorrow. It was 2 a.m. when Isabel sent for the doctor.

What had caused this attack? Not carrying fossils, surely. He'd been much stronger since he'd had regular work and regular meals. Overwork, possibly. Too much teaching, too many classes. He needed to slow down, he knew. Even his bank balance said so. He had opened an account at Westminster Bank earlier in the year. His balance by March was

£50, and he had even been able to send home a check or two to his parents.

But none of that would do any good if he couldn't stay alive. The doctor arrived and iced his chest. He then gave strict instructions to his aunt and his wife. Wells heard them murmuring in the hall. Then he slept till morning. When he awoke, he felt changed. Lighter, somehow, released from his burdens. He pushed himself up on his pillows and looked around at the crisp, clean room. Things felt airy and carefree. He decided he wanted to write a few letters sharing his new perspective. He wrote to Elizabeth Healey, his closest friend from the Normal School, that his teaching days were done. He had Lowson as assistant already, a benefit from when he'd tried to quit the year before. Briggs had enticed him back after the last hemorrhage with the promise of an assistant. But now he was done. Davies could take over easily.

The next day Wells, sitting fully up in bed, received a note. It was a request from his old friend Richard Gregory, who was broke and had obviously not yet heard of Wells' illness. Could he borrow £10, just for a week? It never occurred to Wells to say no. From his sickbed, he dispatched the money. A week later, a grateful note came from Gregory, enclosing £10.

Tears filled his eyes as the note fluttered down onto the coverlet. Why am I crying? thought Wells. I've just survived a hemorrhage, I'm quitting teaching, and I'm brought to tears by Gregory paying me back. He'd made little loans to friends before. No one, he realized, had ever paid him back. He vowed to write that physiography textbook with Gregory as soon as he felt better. It could earn as much money as the one Wells was writing for biology. They'd split it half and half, and that would help his friend. But first, he should lay back and read that book by J. M. Barrie. He wanted to read his early work, before the reviews had gotten so good. He also wanted to write another note to Amy Robbins. He thought about her a lot.

The first week's recuperation was otherwise restful. He was sure he wasn't going to die. But he was hungry, as he had been the first night. His aunt prescribed Valentine's Extract, a meat-based concoction that gave him energy and power, for a full week. It was reputed to be better than Liebig's extract, and doctors recommended it. Aunt Mary mixed it in warm water for him to drink. Valentine's Extract, Wells thought. What would I do without it?

~

The Old Operating Theatre and Herb Garret was just a little out of the way. But I suppose, thought Katherine, Southwark has always been considered a little out of the way. She had somehow ended up on the ground floor of the Shard. There were sandwich-board signs advertising the view from the top, for a fee. She knew the museum was in an old church of some kind. Looking down the street, she saw only the hospital and rows of buildings. As she began walking toward Borough Market, she saw the museum's placard.

Entering the open door, the space ahead of her looked disturbingly modern. There was white lettering on glass doors directly in front of her. Then she saw the sign pointing to the left, to a smaller door. Curiouser and curiouser, she thought. Shall I need to eat or drink something to be small enough to enter the museum?

She ducked through the door and immediately faced a flight of spiral stairs. It would indeed have helped to be smaller. Not for the first time did she wish she were slimmer. The passage upward was narrow, and the stone stairs were narrow, worn, and shallow. A rope, attached occasionally to the wall, was needed to climb up. She passed a tiny room with books, papers, and a computer, as she ascended. Then there was a large step, to the side, onto linoleum. I've made it, she thought, rather breathless. The room was a small gift shop, with a desk. There was no one there.

So, she looked around. Plastic ink pens shaped like syringes. Strange concoctions of sugar labelled like medicine. Books about medieval medical practice. A young woman came in and said, "one ticket?" Katherine paid and was pointed through another tiny doorway.

The Herb Garret was an extraordinary room. It had been the herb-drying attic of St. Thomas's Hospital. A stack of children's activities lay on the wooden trestle table by the top of the stairs. Displays were thickly laid out with traditional herbs, each with a hand-written note explaining its use. She smiled at the meadowsweet, which she herself used for pain. She'd had no idea what the plant looked like. Apparently it was more commonly used for diarrhea and UTIs. There was an anesthesia mask, and a ceramic phrenology head (was that what they were called?), and stories about the Victorian patients.

Across the room and down a ramp was a door of more reasonable size, and Katherine entered the Operating Theatre itself. The room was larger and much lighter than she expected. She was at the bottom of its horseshoe shape, where the patient would have been wheeled in. A skylight let in a milkiness that illuminated every corner. She imagined all the medical students in the seats, looking down at her. What an extraordinary place to be so high up in the building. What an excellent setting for a murder mystery, she thought. The victim, he's in the gallery, sitting up straight. Except he's dead. A ramrod up his behind holds him erect, like a statue. Maybe he's a doctor. Perhaps the family of a dead patient had killed him. Maybe nobody found him for days.

She read that the room had been built in 1822, but in 1862 the hospital had moved. The entrances to this entire area were then blocked, so eventually no one remembered the theatre was there. She would want to set her mystery during the Wellsian era, of course. Could the body be in a blocked-up room? Or perhaps it had been reopened by then.

But no, an informative sign told her. A historian, researching the hospital, had discovered the theatre only recently, in 1956. How was it possible that something so large had been hidden for so long?

I should imagine myself as the patient, she thought. The poor patient, hoping for relief, given oral alcohol and anal tobacco as strong analgesics. There wasn't anything in the way of anesthesia in the 1840s. It was the time of Dickens, and people with tumors in their necks and legs that needed amputating would have it done in here. All the students would take notes as she suffered. Sawdust on the floor would absorb the blood.

It was no use. She saw herself as the doctor, trying to help, working as quickly as possible to avoid the patient experiencing too much pain.

∾

Science is only helpful up to a point, said Wells.

Yes, said Katherine, I've found that too.

They thought I had tuberculosis for the longest time. I suppose now there are tests for that.

Yes, said Katherine, they have tests for a lot of things.

Have you had many of them? he asked

I have, said Katherine. And I've been told the various protocols, had predictions made, told what to do, what would be best.

I was told to rest a lot, he said.

I've never been told that, she said. It's interesting. A rest cure has never been suggested. I suppose in your day you just went to the seaside.

We did, he said. That's why I decided to build my house at Sandgate. I was told it was good for my health, and then I could bicycle all around the area.

Your house, she said, is an elder care residence now. I can't even go see the inside.

You see? said Wells. It was good for healthy living. But I couldn't stay away from London that much. I ended up traveling, then moving back to the city. But I did go on holidays.

I do holidays, said Katherine. Mostly I come and look for you. I'm afraid that isn't what they told me to do.

I didn't always do what doctors said either, said Wells. Except when they told me to move somewhere nice.

～

Katherine was becoming experienced on British trains. In the south, she noticed, people were very quiet and private. They read a newspaper or a book or listened on ear buds. Traveling in pairs at most, they sat three feet apart on benches, and stood two feet apart in queues and in lifts. Personal distance, she recalled. They have quite a bit of personal distance.

As trains moved north, their character changed as people got off and on.

She'd noticed this trend first in Chicago, where she had gone for a conference. While there, she very much wanted to visit the Museum of Science and Industry. The conference hotel was downtown, so she caught the bus to the south side. When she got on, the bus was full of people who were well-dressed, busy, pale-skinned. As the bus moved southward, these people left one or two at a time, and more casually-dressed, sociable, and darker-skinned people got on. By the time she got to the museum, she was the only pale and alone person on the bus. The process reversed itself when she returned later that day.

Segregation in America was well known. During World War II, a film for American servicemen was made called "How to Behave in Britain." Burgess Meredith took the viewer through some helpful tips on how not to be an obnoxious American when stationed in the UK. In one scene, he and a black American serviceman both said goodbye to a British woman on a train. They had been talking on the journey, and she invited them both to her house sometime for tea. Meredith was at pains to point out that although things were "different" at home, soldiers were not at home and should behave accordingly.

To Katherine, the fact that they'd all been chatting amiably on the train meant it was likely a northern journey.

As she traveled on trains from London going northeast, especially, she noticed the shift. As the train moved northward, the quiet, subdued, single people left. The more chatty, sociable people, sometimes in groups of three or four, got on. On a trip to York, a professional-looking man got on, and sat beside her. As she often did, she made an offhand comment. It was usually about the weather, or the crowding, or the difficult seats. Something innocuous. This left the field open to either possible conversation, or a polite reply followed by a return to media intended for private use.

The professional man responded. As conversation progressed, it dawned on him that even though she was American, Katherine was an educated woman. He began to tell her about his trip, to meet with the National Health Service. There was an invention, he said, that would help hospitals and more, might help the world. It cleaned and sterilized surgical instruments during an operation. He paused, seemingly unsure if this was an appropriate topic. She nodded.

"You know what surgical instruments are?" he said. His eyes had that light, expressing deep interest in one's own subject.

"Yes, I come from a medical family," she said. The light got brighter.

"Then you know that during surgery, the instruments get messy and slippery. But what if you can clean, sterilize and dry them as you go? This machine does that."

"That sounds amazing," she said. "That means fewer instruments are needed for a single operation, and less storage space for equipment."

"Exactly! And more. It operates without external power, so it could be used where there isn't electricity. Rural Africa, for example." He handed her his card, and she wished him luck with the NHS.

It occurred to her afterward that this was not the sort of conversation one would have on a southern train.

How do you package a life? Katherine asked. I've been wanting to do that for the last couple of years. Wrap it all up. I even asked a therapist to help me do it. He wasn't willing to help. We'd start and then he'd just revert to talking about now.

There was a point where someone decided to wrap up my life, Wells said. Geoffrey West. Except that his name was really Geoffrey Wells. But I was having none of that. We weren't related. Everyone would think we were. So, I made him change it for my biography.

That's odd, she said. Why was the name West better? You'd already had a child by Rebecca West. Didn't you think people would make that association?

I suppose I must have, he said. Perhaps I didn't care as much about that as my own name. I did cooperate fully with Geoffrey West. A number of my friends had died recently, and I wanted my story told before I was gone.

Is that why, she said, you then wrote your own autobiography?

West's book was fine, said Wells. He helped me remember many things. But then I wanted to write about them myself. Write an autobiography of my own brain. I had grown and changed so much.

I'm very glad you did, said Katherine.

11

It must be official, because it was announced in the *Athenæum*. Walter Low was to be the new editor of the *Educational Times*.

The journal was the official organ of the College of Preceptors, the proverbial feeding hand that Wells so often bit. Founded by a group of private schoolmasters, the College had professionalized teaching, developing standards and offering awards for merit. Levels could be achieved, the highest being the Licentiate. Wells had one of these.

As a close friend, Walter Low had come to Wells with an idea.

The two men had much in common. They had both worked hard to acquire university credentials, only to discover they were suited for little other than coaching potential examinees and doing a bit of teaching. They had both married as the result of romantic visions that remained unrealized. And they both enjoyed arguing, especially about politics. Low's Jewishness provided a continual source of intellectual exchange. Most importantly, both believed that they were destined for more than they had.

Low had proposed his idea as they strolled along Kensington Road. It was a warm evening, and they were there solely because they liked the neighborhood.

"I am the editor now of the *Educational Times*, you know," Low began.

"I do," said Wells, "and best of luck with it."

"They will be paying me," said Low, "£100 a year."

"That seems like a lot," said Wells. "I barely earn half that."

"So that's where my idea comes in," said Low. "Half of that is what I actually earn, for me. The other half I'm supposed to use to pay the contributors to the journal."

"Who are the contributors?" asked Wells.

"That's just it," said Low. "They gave me a list of a few people who have been contributing, but I don't have to use any of them. In fact, it's expected that I will start over, as the new editor."

"Sounds exciting," said Wells. "Who would be good?"

Low was becoming a bit exasperated. His friend wasn't nibbling at the bait. They crossed Exhibition Road, neatly jumping ahead of a turning carriage.

"I was thinking," said Low, "that *you* would be good."

"I'd be delighted to write a few articles for you, old man." said Wells. Low was a year older than Wells, so this was an old joke.

"No," cried Low, "I want you to be *all* the contributors."

"All of them?" Wells stopped suddenly on the pavement in front of the Royal Albert Hall.

"Yes, can't you see?" said Low. "It will save me so much bother. The tedium of correspondence. The difficulty finding people. The writing of checks." He was smiling now.

"Good heavens," said Wells. "Do you think anyone would mind?"

"Who'll know?" said Low.

They made an interesting pair, Low tall and dark, Wells short and bouncy.

"I'll do it," said Wells, "but you must teach me all you know about writing."

"Happy to, young man!" replied Low.

∽

Katherine was back in Cambridge again. I really don't like Cambridge, she thought. I prefer Oxford. She looked around. The river, the beautiful buildings, the students on bicycles, the groups of Chinese tourists. So similar to Oxford, and yet not. It seemed like a copy. Newer, cleaner, but a copy.

A meeting had been set up with a scholar famous for his own study of H. G. Wells. He had kindly agreed, by email, to meet with her. She was a little star struck, and that never worked in her favor. He had asked her to choose the place, so she chose a coffee shop on Trumpington. But when she got there she realized all the seats were small and made of wood. He would surely be an older gentleman, and she wasn't so young herself. The room was also crowded and noisy, but she bought a tea and found a table. The table was very small. When she put her bag on it, she couldn't see its surface any more.

After he arrived, wearing a suit half a size too large, she felt embarrassed asking him to sit in such a place, and after introductions she offered to move somewhere less noisy. He suggested the coffee shop at the Fitzwilliam Museum. She rose, grabbed her bag, and squeezed out after him.

Predictably, the walk to the museum was very rapid. Everyone I've met here, she thought, is at least ten years older than me. And they all walk so fast. She knew she wasn't that weak. She'd been doing more walking herself, and even some aerobic exercising. It didn't seem to be enough. She could sense him slowing politely so she could walk alongside.

The museum had a lot of school children, but not in the coffee area. They ordered, and he insisted on paying for her tea. She had spent the previous day going through some of his earlier works but had been having trouble thinking of a way to converse with someone who knew so much. So, she asked about his sister. He had told her he might not have much time because his sister was in hospital. She had offered another time, but he had insisted this day was fine.

"I may have to take a call," he apologized, "in case I have to go pick her up."

"Oh," said Katherine, "she's all right then? Coming home?"

He didn't answer about her condition, but said they'd agreed she could come home. Katherine looked at his tired eyes, his horn-rimmed glasses, his frown. She couldn't see why anyone would be willing to spend time with an American educator when your sibling was so ill. She felt she should help him, somehow, with her talk. Be a sympathetic ear. But surely that was inappropriate too. Forgetting everything she'd read in his work, she tried to make conversation about Wells. But she couldn't focus, and it became obvious she'd misinterpreted the meeting. She realized afterward, when he was making confused goodbyes, that she'd done it wrong.

She had talked about what she had done, her own research. She had asked politely about anything he happened to mention. But she didn't know anything about him personally, so the sister in the hospital occupied her mind. They had been introduced, through email, by the head of the archive in London. They would have so much to talk about, she had said. She must have told him that Katherine had many questions. Given his experience, he was prepared to be interviewed. But she had no questions for him. She had, regrettably, wasted his time. It was far more embarrassing than small wooden seats or a crowded coffee house.

After he left the museum, she went upstairs to look at the paintings. She loved Annunciations. There was something about the variety of responses the Virgin Mary exhibited that was both comforting and delightful. They varied by era and by artist, in a far more individual way than other Biblical subjects. And the Fitzwilliam, she'd discovered, had more Annunciations than most. Domenico Veneziano's, with the angel kneeling from across the room, and Mary with her head bowed like he's asked her to dance. Spinelo Aretino's, where Mary's looking so seriously at her book that it's like the angel isn't there. The one attributed to Bernart van Orley, where she seems to be meditating in the luxurious interior, while Gabriel executes a one-footed landing from the sky like a gymnast. And Martino di Bartolomeo's, where the angel looks like he's telling a fabulous story, gesticulating madly, while Mary gazes at him like he's crazy.

At least, she thought, I know that conversation didn't go any better.

∿

December 1893

"I'm married, you know," said Wells.

Amy looked up from her drawing. Her lovely face shined up at him.

"I know," she said, "and I know how you feel about marriage." She returned to her work.

The reviews were in for his biology textbook. Most had been favorable, but several had mentioned the poor quality of the drawings. Wells had done them all himself. He'd taught scientific drawing and written about its importance in the curriculum. He had felt they were good enough. His reviewers felt otherwise.

Amy had graciously agreed to redraw all the diagrams for the next edition. She was talented. Her shading and precision made all the illustrations more clear. Her splayed frog was particularly good. Any scholar working at any kitchen table would be able to follow along and compare. And Wells had long promoted the value of laboratory work. She wouldn't be credited, of course. But everyone would know that she was the artist.

They were in the laboratory at Red Lion Square. He'd known her for a year, and loved her for almost that long, although he hadn't wanted to admit it.

"Look," he said, taking the pen out of her hand.

"At what?" She grinned.

"Do you remember when I wrote you last summer, when I was ill?"

"Oh yes," she said. "I kept all your letters." She grabbed for the pen, but he put it behind his back.

"Aunt Mary was sick, and you were studying so hard. Then you passed your examination, and I could only congratulate you by letter. And I advised you to stay with Biology."

"You sounded quite like a grandfather," said Amy.

"I tried not to write anything that Isabel or Aunt Mary couldn't see. But then there was last week."

"I remember last week," Amy laughed.

"When we were at your house, she could see it. You and I. Or hear it, anyway. Isabel's always been terribly jealous of anyone who could excite me with conversation."

"Your wife is lovely, H. G."

"She is. And I still love her. But she's made it easy for me. She put it to me last night."

Amy frowned. "Put what to you?"

"She said I must give up my friendship with you. If I don't, she'll leave me."

Amy reached for the pen, and Wells gave it back. There was a long pause. The evening light was shining through the tall laboratory windows. It was very quiet. Everyone had gone home hours ago.

"Because we talk well together?"

"Because she sees that I love you."

"And so you do." She began scratching with her pen at a scrap of paper, her face intent.

"I want to be with you. I want to get a divorce and be with you."

A slow smile, still looking at the paper. The ink was seeping through. "In that order?"

"Please be serious. I want us to live together. I am writing more now. Simmons wrote that amazing review, so the textbook is selling. I have some money. It won't be fancy. Or easy. But together, you and I…"

"Together you and I will die of consumption." She coughed.

"Possibly. But think of all the things we could do in the meantime."

"I could save your book with my wonderful drawings."

"You are!" he said. "And you could inspire me, and I could inspire you, and I'd see you every morning at the breakfast table, and we'd share our dreams."

Amy looked out the window.

"Could we have a cat?" she said.

"We could have a cat," he said, his eyes twinkling.

"Then all right," said Amy.

∽

The problems with writing a book about you, she said, are multiple.

Really? he said. I would have thought I'm an excellent subject.

You are, which is why everything has already been written. Books and articles about you number in the hundreds.

Deservedly, he said, nodding.

But I was once advised, she said, that if I did write about you I wouldn't be able to avoid the problem of sex.

Ah, yes, he said. Sex was a problem. I take it sex is still a problem?

The problem, she said, isn't really sex. It's that people nowadays, especially in America, take it quite seriously. Talking about it openly isn't really possible.

During my day, he said, it wasn't either. Victorian era, you know.

These days, she said, it isn't mere prudishness. It's that sex has been used to oppress women. So many women are coming forward to talk about being sexually manipulated or abused by powerful men. I've been told it's a poor time to write about you for that reason.

I didn't oppress anyone, he said.

I know, she said. But you weren't exactly typically Victorian either.

Ah, he said. The first problem then would be my marriage and finding Jane.

I'm afraid so, she said. You married your own cousin, which I suppose can be overlooked. But then you fell in love with your student and left your wife.

It wasn't that simple, he said. Isabel and I did try to make a go of it, but it was no use. She didn't understand my brain, how I think, how I dream. I didn't abandon her. I sent her money once I could, and always helped her. We stayed friends.

I think, she said, people might be able to overlook the divorce. They might be able to appreciate a happier marriage. But later in your life, the affairs, the illegitimate children, the woman who tried to commit suicide over you. These things are not as easy to explain away.

Well, he said, in that case I don't think we're talking about mere prudishness in my life either. I believed in free love. I did not dissemble on the issue. At several points I thought my needs would require me to leave Jane. I always called her Jane, you know, even though her name was Amy -- it was our little joke. I am forever grateful that she did not allow us to separate, but did allow me to do as I wished. Once she even took my lover and her child into her home. Jane was a very intelligent woman. I miss her every day.

I do understand, she said. Had I been able, my life would have been similar. Even as it is, I've had enough lovers that people remember me as a much more interesting person than I am now. I was not as knowledgeable in those days, but how do we gain knowledge?

Through experience, he said.

Exactly, she said. I've had many experiences. Perhaps not enough to last a lifetime. But I learned so much. I learned art and design working in theatre. Music through playing drums in a band. Literature through wonderful books in the public library. And love in so many places. Parked cars on hilltops, backstage among the costumes, crowded parking garages, private spaces where I've touched the moon and the stars.

I touched them too, he said. And sometimes, they touched me back.

∽

Books were, of course, terribly important. For Katherine, each trip meant more book shopping. She had decided that her personal library lacked many of the classics. The nineteenth century should not be a gap, given the work she was doing.

At first she set out to buy only editions published during the author's lifetime. This proved tricky, and she had already made several mistakes ordering online. She'd paid $40 for a copy of *The Wheels of Chance*, only to have it arrive moldy and foxed. (She had learned that "foxing" meant the spots that looked like coffee stains on book pages.) Despite her purchase of book cleaning supplies and magic erasers, poorly kept books never really looked nice.

And she wanted her shelves to look nice, like her image of a real library. If one reads current fiction, it's fine to have the shelves full of shiny photographic covers. But if one is collecting nineteenth-century books to actually read, they should look the part.

Katherine also wanted a book to feel right. Since she usually read fiction in bed, the book needed to be small enough that dropping it wouldn't injure her head. But it had to be hardcover to maintain its gravitas, and to hold her booklight. This meant smaller format books. She became well-versed in Everyman's Library and Collins Classics. To keep the small volumes inexpensive, much text had been crammed on every page. She found this satisfying, especially when compared to modern fiction. The huge tomes, with so few words on each page, were such a waste of paper. Why all the white space? These weren't Tolstoy. You didn't need space to take notes.

Each trip to England meant journeys to second-hand bookstores. She already had favorites. Skoob in Bloomsbury. Oxfam books in Durham. Oxfam bookstores anywhere, really.

Promises of "book towns," bookshop trail maps, were enticing, but often wrong. Sedbergh, for example, called itself Book Town. Enchanted, Katherine had asked her friend Linda to take her there. Besides, it meant a drive through the Dales, always a treat. There seemed to be a lot of signs saying Books. This was promising. Linda parked the car near a tea shop.

They began walking the small town. It was lovely. The day was sunny, with a breeze. You could see the green hills and dales from many places. They stopped at the first place with a sign. It was a charity shop, with clothes and hats. At the back there was a wall with books. Not very many, but a couple of local interest. On to the next. Again, quite a bit of small furniture and hand-made baskets and woolly hats. A couple of shelves on the side wall with some books. Books! said a sign. This one was closed. They peered in at the windows and saw one lonely bookshelf half-hidden behind the till.

There was a much bigger sign at the bottom of a road. They followed its arrow, climbing the hill to a large building. Oh, this will be better, thought Katherine. The building was old and had been lovingly refurbished. Up on the hill, it had a lovely view of the town and the dales beyond. There was even a porch with chairs, just the place to sit and read. But inside, the room was full of clothing racks. This wasn't a charity shop. All the jackets and coats and socks were handmade locally. The woman welcomed them and told them all about these items, and why they were so wonderful. Linda chatted amiably, while Katherine went into other rooms. They were all quite large, with few items in them. Katherine entered the furthest room, at the end. There, to her right, almost hiding beside the doorway, was a small white bookshelf. It looked quite bereft. The two little shelves of books had little of interest, nothing older than 1975.

In the long run, only the very large Westwood Books was worthwhile. Rows of small editions in the huge back room. Piles of sheet music, whole collections purchased by lot, more foxing than you could shake a stick at. A section of rarer books at the front, with more small editions crowding a little shelf next to the till. This was more like it.

But what to do after buying all these books? They might fit in her suitcase but would add too much weight. So, she posted them back home.

Long ago (the 1980s) this had been a wonderful thing to do. The Post Office would help her put everything in the right box and charge a "printed matter" rate. The boxes took forever to arrive (one box took two months) but it was worth it. She could anticipate their arrival.

But things change. Here she was in Chelsea, at the Pensioners' Hospital. They had a post office. She had already discovered that there was no such thing as a book rate anymore. The Royal Post Office website listed the prices by kilogram. She made sure her little box was under five kilograms, and her books well padded, by adding in two packages of Marks and Spencer underwear. White cotton. But she hadn't had any packing tape.

The pensioner at the desk (it was so nice to be among people older than she was) was very helpful. He had kind eyes and a large grey moustache.

"Is it printed matter?" he asked.

"Well, yes," she said, "mostly. But I thought there wasn't a printed matter rate anymore?"

"Oh, well, let me see. Henry?" he called to the pensioner in the other room.

"Yes, Jim?"

"There is a special rate for printed matter in a small box, yes?"

Henry came over, slowly.

"Well, let's see. I think there may be one if it's under five kilograms."

"Thank you," she said, "but the website said there was just a single price for anything under five kilograms."

"Is it under five kilograms?" She confirmed it was.

Henry started to come around the desk.

"Steady on, there," said Jim, "you're only on the till."

It was then Katherine noticed that Jim had an official Post Office uniform, but Henry had the typical pensioners' scarlet coat.

"Well, all right then," said Henry, taking no offense, "check the black book."

The book was duly checked.

"All right," said Jim, as if the serious negotiations were about to commence, "is it only printed matter?"

"Um, no," said Katherine.

"What else is in there?"

"Um, some theatre programs, and some blank paper, and…" She wouldn't blush. This was ridiculous.

"Right. Well if you want the printed matter rate, you'll need to remove anything that isn't printed matter."

So with both pensioners looking on, Katherine opened the box, and removed the very obvious packages of M&S knickers. Both men tried hard not to smile.

"Um…these were here to keep the books from knocking each other about," she said quietly.

"Yesss. Henry, do you still have that newspaper from yesterday?"

Henry set off into the other room to find it.

"Here on holiday, are you?" asked Jim. This was probably the most common question Katherine got, and she relaxed now that they were on more typical ground.

"For part of my trip," she said. "I'm also here to do some historical research."

Jim nodded wisely, and Katherine knew what he was thinking. Every British person to whom she mentioned "research" assumed she was an American looking into her British family history. But Katherine had no family history in England. She didn't think, however, that most people would be that interested in young Wells.

Jim packed up the books with crumpled newspaper ("printed matter," he said), and provided tape. Katherine thanked them both, purchased a postcard and a little pin of a Chelsea pensioner, and went to visit the Chelsea Physic

Garden. I wonder whether they have an herb for embarrassment, she thought.

～

But what about history? she asked. In your early writings about teaching, you denigrated history. It was one of the subjects you recommended not teaching to young people, to make room for science.

While that is true, he said, it was because it was so poorly taught. All those names and dates, lists and outlines. That isn't history at all. It's record-keeping.

So, as with everything else, eventually you wrote your own.

I did, he said. And I did it properly. The story of mankind in readable form.

But I am a historian, she said. I would say that history is like many other fields of knowledge. It is a canvas upon which the historian paints his own wishes and dreams.

That is true, he said. And in my case, it was the idea that there could be a coherent narrative, a unification of history. Science, to me, was always about unity.

I remember you wrote about that, she said. Especially when you wrote about evolution. What one ultimately learns from comparing forms and their history, you implied, is that everything forms a natural unity.

And it is natural, he said. Not supernatural, not caused by God.

So, for you, she said, science was your canvas. You wrote your dreams upon it.

Not at all, he said. Science was reality. What man did with it, that was where dreams came in. And nightmares too.

I wonder now, she said, about personal history, since I am faced with my own. Science is impersonal. There is no emotional investment in evolution, or atoms, or nebulae. But so many people want to make history personal. They want their own story to matter.

135

It only matters to them, he said. Because it isn't history at all. It's memory.

~

Her memories about enjoying places were often about walking. Her hometown in the middle of California, which suffered from extreme high temperatures in summer and bone-chilling fog in winter, was not a place to walk. Holidays were freeing not only in their separation from work, but in their physical exhilaration. Even if it was a slow, quiet exhilaration.

Katherine had never been one for exercise. She knew it was good for you, and as a child she had ridden a bicycle. She'd lost three teeth turning too sharply speeding down the hill behind her house. She had seen the film *The Turning Point* and had taken ballet. Her pear shape, knock knees, and uncertain balance put paid to that idea. As an adult, she forced herself to go to Jazzercise classes and undertake gym programs. She hated every minute of it. Dancing was the only exception, if one didn't count sex, the only exercise that seemed worth the trouble. When dancing got difficult that too became a chore. As she aged there were no places to dance unless you were in it for the drinking. She wasn't. And love, however exciting and athletic it was at first, always faded, if it didn't explode first.

Her family had gone to Hawai'i a few times when she was a teenager, and she would surprise herself walking for miles along the beach. She walked from Ka'anapali to Lahaina and returned sunburned and content. On a bus trip in the Canadian Rockies, she'd walked for hours around Lake Louise, utterly alone, and felt at peace. Every new city, over the years, the first thing she'd done was go for a long walk. To get my bearings, she thought. She'd been so pleased to discover that she could walk for many miles without tiring, so long as the place was interesting.

One needn't decide where one was going when walking. One could just go and return at leisure. And along the way, unlike in her hometown, there would be things to see:

buildings, rivers, people, flowers. And one could think, or not, as one wished. A long, complex conversation with oneself could best happen on a walk.

When the pain was minimal, and she was able to dream happily, she'd go for a walk in her mind. Durham was always a favorite. Down across Elvet Bridge, past the smallest gin bar in the world, up to the fork in the road where broad steps went upward. At that point, she could turn left and go up Saddler Street, past the tapas restaurant and Bill's, up toward the castle and across Palace Green to the cathedral. Or she could turn right and go past Gregg's and the bank machines into Market Square, then left again down the hill where all the shops changed so often. Then, just before the restaurant near the bridge, down the steps to the river walk. Going straight, one walked along the river, with occasional benches if needed, among the trees. Keep going and one came to the fulling mill, which she always touched for luck. Then past the monument where students met to drink, right before Prebends Bridge. So many options from that point. To the left up the hill around the back of the cathedral through the colleges. Across the bridge and down by the famous view of the mill. Onward to the other side of town with the hills of houses overlooked by the railway bridge.

Knowing that others had walked in the same place grounded her in the flow of humanity. She'd felt that everywhere, but especially in Europe. Walking Montmartre in Paris, getting lost among the small streets of Venice, walking near the walls in Orvieto. Strolling along the Embankment in London, across the Jubilee Bridge to Southwark, back across at Westminster. Old places, strong places. Places where it was all right to be a temporary being, a person just passing through. One's ultimate absence would scarce be noticed by slippery cobbled streets, by post-modern skyscrapers next to medieval churches, by brutalist architecture replacing buildings that had burned in the Great Fire. California had its Spanish and Indian heritage, but she'd never felt it under her feet. In England, she heard the voices in the ground. They made it acceptable to be transient.

12

In the early days of her web-based teaching adventures, Katherine had found herself a mentor. He had not known he was her mentor. Gary Benson was an enthusiastic online educator. He had developed a philosophy of teaching over the internet and published a series of web pages on his thoughts and techniques. There were no blogs then.

Not accustomed yet to reading on the screen, and not owning an expensive screen where that would be easier, she printed all of Benson's work. He seemed to know, even early in the years of the web, what this new technology meant for education. Even more, he knew how to use it gently, to teach. Balancing technology and humanity was the key, he had taught her. She read and learned and emailed him once to ask a question. He answered her kindly. Then one day, she learned he had died. Learned it days afterward, online. It was a kitchen floor death, sudden, like Spencer Tracy.

He had never known how important he was to her, and she had never met him. But she felt a creeping sadness and searched the internet to find reports of his death. His work was all still online. Soon it would be taken down. Later a Facebook memorial page would appear. He was not a movie star, not a celebrity. How could she feel so strongly about his demise?

Wisdom, said her therapist. He had counseled her on and off for twenty-five years, and was saying goodbye. You have achieved much in the way of street smarts, and kindness, and peacefulness. All you need now is wisdom.

The things people say when they're leaving, she thought. Those parting lines. She had heard a few. "I feel like this is the end," one lover had said over the phone. "That's because it is," she had replied. Perhaps he still remembered her. Perhaps not. Perhaps this was the wisdom she was supposed to acquire. As a very young soul, she doubted that such wisdom would be possible. There simply wouldn't be time.

One needs the long view, she knew. In the early days of Facebook she thought that she might look up everyone from her childhood she could remember. But many beat her to it. She got a friend request from a girl who had stood on the corner and tormented her every morning as she walked to elementary school. Then another from a boy from junior high with whom she had been madly in love, but who had ignored her and went off with her friend. She had stopped attending high school reunions because she did not remember people the way they remembered her. And many she did not remember at all, even though she had written stories about them in the school newspaper. But she remembered those who had hurt her, and here they were wanting to be her "friend." Instead, she began friending people she really had liked. Then she realized they didn't remember her, in the same way that she didn't remember the others. It seemed like a cocktail party of ghosts and illusions. An on-screen collection of imaginary friends.

She had worked hard as an online teacher to mitigate that distance of the internet, to create environments for learning. The truth was that she loved the removal from people. In the classroom, she was expected to remember students' names. Hundreds, later thousands of students, in sets of forty, passing through each term. I cannot remember your names, she told them. It's because I'm a historian. My brain is full of dead people. I'm sorry, but I can't lose Thomas Jefferson for you.

༄

The new boarding house wasn't much to look at. It stretched upward out of Eardley Road, and when you looked up at it, it seemed to lean against the sky at an odd angle. But all the houses on that side of the street looked like that.

H.G. and Jane, for whom he had left his first wife, had moved there from Mornington Road. Her given name was Amy Catherine, but he liked calling her Jane.

"I'm going to work," he said to Jane, "on fixing up those stories I wrote for the *Science Schools Journal*. 'The Chronic Argonauts' will be a novel, and this time, I'll get it published. It will be called *The Time Traveller.*"

"Will it," said Jane. She was darning his sock.

His *Text-book of Biology* had been published the previous year, and the physiography book with Gregory also, but this was not what he wanted. Jane had awakened in him bigger dreams. She was studying for her biology examinations, sharing ideas at the breakfast table, accepting his overtures at night. She organized his calendar, kept track of friends, and was a marvelous hostess. So many false starts, but he knew he was on the verge of success.

"You know," he said to Jane, "I have been fired up about writing since I read Barrie's book *When a Man's Single*. No need to write about large scientific and philosophical ideas. I can just write stories, invent tales about small, trivial things."

"Can you," said Jane. She bit off the thread in her teeth.

"You," he said grandly to Jane, "will improve your health, and study for your examinations. We'll go for walks and collect specimens. It's a shame they're no longer taking my stories in the *Pall Mall Budget*. But the divorce papers are here at last, so soon . . . I need to work on something big that will make us some money, better than all those articles, and a good deal less important."

It was summer, and he was still writing late into the night when the landlady found out about the divorce, which meant the couple she was hosting were not married. She began to complain incessantly about them, to them, and around them. They had to move. Wells frantically wrote every day, trying to finish what had been *The Time Traveller* but was now *The Time Machine*. Jane went off each day to look for a better place for them to live. She was asked awkward questions and returned tired.

One day she came home pleased.

"I've done it," she said. "The answer is to move backward rather than forward."

"I'm sorry?" Wells said, distracted. "Have you found us a place? That woman interrupted me three times today asking when we will go and make her house respectable again."

"Yes," said Jane, "I've found a place. You'll be pleased. It will seem rather familiar."

Wells frowned.

"We're going back to Mornington Road."

"Sorry?" he said again. "There's another flat free in Mornington Road?"

"Better," she said, grinning. "It's our old flat, number 12, available again, with Mrs. Lewis, just like before!"

Wells was delighted. Mrs. Lewis had fussed over them, the flat was close to the heart of London, and by winter he'd be divorced and they could marry. He worked and Jane packed, while the landlady continued complaining.

Three days before they were to go, a letter arrived. It was from William Henley. He was starting a new literary journal, *The New Review*. He wanted "The Time Machine" to feature in the first issues as a series. He'd pay £100 in advance.

"A hundred pounds!" Wells said to Jane, "Can you believe it? And I got another note from Henry Cust, who knows Henley, of course. He wants me to start up again for the *Pall Mall Gazette*, with all my articles signed this time."

Jane's eyes glittered.

"I have news too," she said. "Mother is going to north London to live with her friends."

A flat to themselves. Paid and signed writings in the offing. No more marking papers and carrying fossils. Money to send home to his parents. They would finally start their lives as author and amanuensis. He took her to bed at once.

∽

I don't want to go in, thought Katherine. Why should I? If it's bad news, there will be decisions. These decisions are supposed to be made by me. But they won't. Everyone else's feelings will have to be considered.

Medical waiting rooms were a purgatory that now terrified her. I'm from a medical family, she thought. But the character of all this has changed.

In my day, said Wells from the seat next to her, the doctor came to the house.

Yes, she said quietly. But no one nowadays is impressed by the level of medical care they provided.

I was, he said. That icing of my chest was nothing short of brilliant.

It's funny, she said. We have more ice now, too.

I have faith in science, he said. It must be better now.

Burn, cut, or poison, said Katherine. That's all they can do. It's no better than ancient Egypt.

Are you saying my vision of rational medicine did not, as they say in the West, pan out?

Certainly not yet, she said.

The nurse called her name.

∽

At the Chelsea Physic Garden, and at the Old Operating Theatre, she had seen many herbs and their uses. This knowledge was now known to so few. Perhaps other knowledge should be revived or reclaimed, she thought. She'd gotten into a discussion about it at the Beamish Open Air Museum. The trip out there was her first bus ride from Durham. She was a bit nervous going so far away on a bus and kept checking the schedule to make sure she could get back.

She hadn't realized what a big place it was. This was unfortunate, because she was quite tired that day. It was her first trip over alone, and she hadn't realized that it may have been too soon to travel. So she took it very slowly, and used the antique bus and tram to see it all.

The Victorian town, naturally, was most fascinating and most crowded with visitors. She was primarily interested in the apothecary shop. Before she'd decided on Wells for her project, she had considering researching Victorian medicine as a way to get to England. She'd bought the Shire book and done some preliminary investigation. She was intrigued with all the items on display.

There were some ceramic items, shaped almost like vases, but broadening near the top. She asked the attendant, who was posing as apothecary for the visitors.

"Hello. May I ask, what is this for?"

"It's a vaporizer. For inhaling."

The man was young and might have been a university student. This would be a good job for a student, she thought.

"What," she said, "did they inhale?"

He looked surprised.

"It's for lung problems."

"Yes, I mean what was inhaled through this?"

"Let me get my book," he said, a bit excited, "let's find out! Here's some of the recommendations for lung conditions," he said, and handed her the book with its page opened.

She read about all the lung disorders that could be cured by inhaling creosote.

"Goodness," she said, "it's for creosote."

He nodded sagely. "Yes, they used many toxic things back then. Thank heavens for modern medicine."

Now that, thought Katherine, is not at all in character.

"Surely," she said, "it must have worked? I mean, people wouldn't have continued doing it if it didn't do something beneficial."

"Oh. I suppose, but still…"

"And perhaps if you were, say, dying of consumption, a bit of creosote might be curative or helpful, and you wouldn't really care if it was dangerous."

"True," he said, looking annoyed now. "Is there anything else I can help you with?"

∼

Why, said Wells, is opium so hard to obtain now? So many of the women I knew had a bottle of laudanum by their bedside.

And they abused it, she said. Women were so restricted in what they could do, they took the opium even when they weren't in pain. They became addicted to it. And now, in my country, it's very difficult to get a doctor to give you any. My second surgery, I had to beg for it. The new and improved drug they gave me instead did nothing.

The level of man's pain, Wells said, should not depend on the mercy of doctors.

No, Katherine said, nor woman's either. But I'm afraid it does.

∼

British Airways could not complete your check-in online.
Please contact the airline to confirm proper identification.

Katherine double-checked everything. Passport number, address, name. All was correct. This had never happened. What was wrong? She was due to return to California the next day. She was tired. She was particularly tired of Marylebone and sitting here at Bill's Restaurant. It was raining. She couldn't get the server's attention to get more hot water for her tea.

It's because I'm solo, thought Katherine. Seated at the back, next to the toilets. Ignored. It was a Friday morning, and all the tables around her were full. You'd think, she thought, that if they wanted me to leave they'd serve me with more alacrity. She called British Airways.

"We cannot confirm your passport number," they said, "so you cannot travel."

"What?" said Katherine. "What do you mean? It's a return ticket. My passport was fine for coming here."

"We're sorry. The State Department says you cannot be confirmed for travel."

"What am I supposed to do? I have my passport right here. It's valid. Doesn't expire for two more years."

I should have known something like this would happen, she thought. It's the President. He's messed up all our relationships with other countries. Now he won't let me go home.

"You might try contacting the State Department in the U.S."

It was 6 a.m. in Washington. Fine. She'd go to the Natural History Museum and call them later. The Natural History Museum in South Kensington, and the Victorian and Albert Museum next door, were located at the old site of Wells' classes at the Normal School. She could take photos of the Cole building, which used to contain the laboratory classes.

It was 2 p.m. London time when she contacted Washington, and another half hour before reaching a person who could help. The person she needed to talk to would come in to the office in two hours, she was told. She went and looked at the dinosaur skeletons, then called again. 4 p.m. London time. Another half hour to talk with someone who could actually help. The dinosaurs were starting to leer at her.

"You'll need to go to the American Embassy to have your passport confirmed."

She panicked. It was 4:30. 16:30, she corrected herself, automatically. The hall of the museum suddenly seemed horribly crowded and confusing. Where was the American Embassy? She'd never needed to know. She tried Google Maps, but her phone battery was running low and the map wouldn't load. Around her, groups of school children swarmed. What do I do? They'll close at 5, I'm sure. 17:00, that is. She hurried to the shop, to try to ask someone. Queues at the tills were full. She looked around for a guard. Just schoolchildren. Lots of them.

She rushed outside, ran for a cab. The rain was coming down in sheets.

"Where to, in all this rain, then?" said the cabbie. Local, she thought. London.

"Do you know where the American Embassy is?"

"Of course," he said. "It's in St. James."

"Can you take me there, please? I'm in a hurry."

He struggled to turn the taxi around on the strange paved area between the museums. This used to be a street, surely? She checked her phone again. No maps. Low battery.

It was five minutes to closing when she ran up to the outbuilding of the Embassy.

"Please, you must help me," she said. "My airline won't let me travel tomorrow. They say they can't confirm my passport."

"I'm sorry," said the uniform, "we're about to close. You'll have to come back on Monday."

Katherine felt the panic rising up into her throat. "I can't," she said, "my flight's tomorrow." She held out her passport, desperately. The uniform looked at it. "It's fine — it hasn't expired. You'll need to contact the airline."

"I did that," said Katherine. "They're the ones who say they can't let me fly."

"I'm sorry, but you'll have to come back on Monday."

Katherine slumped out into the rain. People in business suits were pouring out of the Embassy, going home. The panic rose into her face. She started to cry. I'm an American, she thought. I need to go home. I don't want to die here. I thought about dying here, I considered it, and now I'm deciding that I don't want to.

The rain was heavy, and she leaned against the outbuilding where she'd come out. Huddled against the wall was a gray man in a floppy hat.

"Hey, love," he said in a thick Northern accent, "what's wrong?" He had very few teeth, and his clothes were good quality, but old and stained. He wore a fetching red scarf around his hat.

"I can't get home," she said, "and they won't help me and they're closed."

"Where's home then?"

"California."

"Well, it could be worse," he said, "I've been here every day for three weeks. They won't let me go to the States to see my family. My daughter is ill. She may be dying."

Katherine wiped her nose. "I'm so sorry," she said. She started to realize he may have been there more than every day. He may have been there nights too. He didn't look like he had anywhere else to go. And here he was, trying to help her.

"But you can't get home," he said. "What are you going to do?"

"I don't know," she sniffled. "Find somewhere to stay till Monday, I suppose. This is going to cost a fortune. And I still don't know what could be wrong with my passport."

"Do you need some money?" he said. He began fishing in numerous pockets, pulling out grubby fivers.

"Oh no," she said, horrified that he would give her something he obviously had so little of. "I have some money. I'm all right, really. Are you all right, though?"

"Oh yes," he said, pushing the bills back to the bottom of a pocket. "I just miss them so much. My daughter has two little girls. They've only met their granddad once. I'll be all right."

"Me too," she said. "I'd better go sort out what to do."

He smiled a gappy smile. "You take care, love," he said.

"You too," she said, and began walking back toward Marylebone. She thought about how kind he'd been. The buses were full. The taxis were full. She walked in the rain all the way. Got back to the flat. They won't let me stay, she thought. This will cost hundreds, maybe thousands, to change the ticket. It was so hard to save just to come here.

Okay, she thought. Stop crying and be resourceful. I still have one unused day on my rail pass. I could use it to get to the airport and argue with British Airways in person. They'll be open, at least. She kept walking, to Paddington. Used her ticket on the Express. Terminal 5. Found a British Airways attendant at the kiosk and told her the problem. She was directed to the Customer Service Inquiries counter.

"Hello," said Katherine. "I need some help. I cannot check in online because it says there's a problem with my passport." She wanted to say: please help me, I went to the Embassy, and it was raining, and they wouldn't help, and it's closed till Monday, and I started to cry, and a nice man talked to me, and this will cost me thousands, and I didn't even care that much about being American until I wanted to go home, and…

"May I have your passport and reservation number, please?"

She was blonde, and tall, and her British Airways uniform was very crisp, red and blue scarf and all. Every hair lacquered in place. She looks so fresh, Katherine thought. Must not have been out in the rain.

The woman tapped on the computer for a long time.

"Everything's in order," she said, handing back the passport. "Shall I print out your boarding pass for tomorrow?"

"Yes, please," said Katherine. And the tears started again.

∿

The hospital machines beeped repeatedly. No alarms, just a steady beating.

I wonder, he said, how I shall die.

Don't interrupt me. Can't you see I'm dying? she said.

I'm sorry, he said. Shall I leave?

No, she said. That's how you'll die. A few days before, one of your biographers came to your house. He was so enthusiastic about meeting you, as everyone was. Especially once the war was over. He kept asking you questions. And you said, don't interrupt me. Can't you see I'm dying?

That's depressing, he said.

Well, it's certainly not as impressive as Oscar Wilde. Either that wallpaper goes, or I do.

I don't think he said that, said Wells.

Perhaps he was talking about the curtains then.

No curtains in here, said Wells.

In a sense, she said, my curtain is.

He sat in thought for a moment.

My work, he said, it will be volumes, won't it?

Yes, she said. It will. And it will go in and out of fashion. They'll make your novels into movies. Then they'll say you were a eugenicist.

I was, he said. But only to get a rise out of people. It took me awhile to realize that was something I shouldn't be playing with. Did a lot over the years to undo that.

And, she said, they'll say you were a cad. Left women behind you like blown roses.

Not likely, he said. I love women.

What, she said, do you suppose they'll say about me?

Wells smiled, but said nothing.

Author's Notes

Anyone writing about the past will naturally be asked about the historical accuracy of their novel. The scenes with young H. G. Wells are imagined, but the people and circumstances have been carefully researched.

Although it is impossible to know whether Wells took young A. A. Milne on the trip to the zoo, he did take classes of boys when Alan was a student at Henley House. Alan's marks were published in the Henley House School Magazine, and were indeed poor compared to his brothers'.

Mrs. Allin did help Wells get his job at Midhurst Grammar School, as her great-granddaughter would confirm in *Midhurst Magazine*, Autumn 2019.

While I'm not sure who took the photograph of Wells with the gorilla skeleton, the skeleton resides at the Grant Museum of Zoology at University College London, and has been moved from a prize position in its own cabinet to more crowded quarters with other specimens.

Wells really did rename his wife Jane, had a cat named Mr. Peter Wells who treated certain visitors with disdain, and studied hard to be a science teacher.

William Briggs did found the University Correspondence College, which served students studying for the exams at the University of London until the 1960s.

The pregnancies of Ada Briggs and Mrs. Allin, and their family circumstances, are accurate, and the timeline exact.

Wells did publish a physiography textbook with R. A. Gregory.

Wells published over seventy-five articles on science teaching before writing *The Time Machine*. He was inspired by J. M. Barrie's *When a Man's Single* to write fiction professionally. Among his many prophecies about the future, Wells did conceive of the idea of the World Brain, and the internet has been considered the modern realization of his concept.

Acknowledgements

This was the book that had to be written, and I thank those who put up with my midnight writing sessions and listened to me read scenes aloud (David, Taylor, and Sarah), those who listened to me talk about Wells for hours (my parents), and those who read drafts and gave me feedback (Erika, Jane, Jenny, John, and Dale).

There are also those who helped, directly or unknowingly, with the research for the project behind this novella: Carly at the Victoria and Albert Museum Archives, Simon Wheeler at Wheeler's Bookshop in Midhurst, Wells's biographers, the H.G. Wells Society, Ros Morpeth at the National Extension College, the young man at the Bodleian Library desk who offered me a paper knife, Simon James and the Palace Green Library, the Midhurst Historical Society, the volunteers at Uppark House, and the flight attendants on British Airways' A380 who bring endless cups of tea.

It may be unusual to acknowledge places, but inspiration came from visiting the back stairs at the Cole Building at the V&A; South Pond, Wheeler's Bookshop, and Knockhundred Row in Midhurst; the carpark that used to be Briggs' University Correspondence College in Cambridge; Wells's various haunts around Sussex; and the Oxford Union.

And a last thank you to H.G. Wells, whose life as a young man has fascinated me since I first found out he taught correspondence courses in biology while I was teaching online classes in history.

Lightning Source UK Ltd.
Milton Keynes UK
UKHW010639280122
397869UK00002B/310